THE ELDER BROTHERS AND THE PADSTOW CRYSTALS

THE ELDER BROTHERS AND THE PADSTOW CRYSTALS

Written by
C.J. Elgert

iUniverse, Inc.

New York   Bloomington

The Elder Brothers and the Padstow Crystals

iUniverse books may be ordered through booksellers or by contacting:

iUniverse
1663 Liberty Drive
Bloomington, IN 47403
www.iuniverse.com
1-800-Authors (1-800-288-4677)

Because of the dynamic nature of the Internet, any Web addresses or
links contained in this book may have changed since publication and
may no longer be valid. This is a work of fiction. All of the characters,
names, incidents, organizations, and dialogue in this novel are either
the products of the author's imagination or are used fictitiously.

ISBN: 978-1-4401-7676-0 (pbk)
ISBN: 978-1-4401-7677-7 (ebk)
ISBN: 978-1-4401-7678-4 (hbk)

Printed in the United States of America

iUniverse rev. date: 10/02/2009

Dedicated to

my two boys Jamie and Nicky

who inspired me with their imaginations

and their fighting

Chapter One

The Disappearance

It didn't seem fair! Why should it happen to them, they hadn't done anything really bad, just the normal kids stuff, maybe a bit too much bickering and maybe, Jamie thought, he had been a bit of a bully to his kid brother. But Nicky was *so* annoying!

Jamie and Nicky were standing on a chilly platform at Paddington station waiting for the train that would take them to their aunt's home, they were going to stay with her until their parents had been found.

It seemed so long ago now, the last day they were all together, but Jamie remembered it clearly. The sun had come out after a morning of rain and his dad had suggested they go for a bike ride. Jamie smiled as he remembered challenging his dad to a race when they reached the park; if he beat his dad, his dad would have to buy him and Nicky a coke and a bag of crisps; if his dad beat him, he promised not to fight with Nicky for two days. Of course, he had won and they had sat down on the park bench and watched some teenagers playing football while they enjoyed their treat. Nicky kept teasing their dad about getting old and not being able to beat Jamie anymore. On the way home they had picked up a bunch of spring flowers for their mum, a little treat because she had to stay home to finish the housework.

When they arrived home their favourite dinner of roast beef and Yorkshire pudding was waiting for them. Everything seemed so perfect, everyone was happy, they had played a game of Skip Bo and were having so much fun teasing their dad about the way he was playing that they didn't notice that their mum was down to her last couple of cards until it was too late and she beat them by 365 points. His parents had promised that they could continue the game after they had done their homework the next day.

But that was the day everything changed.

That was a week ago, though it seemed so much longer. They had come home from school and were surprised to find that their mum wasn't home as she usually was. Not really concerned by this, they dropped their school stuff and got out of their school uniforms and went out to play with their friends, but by six o'clock, when their friends had gone in for supper and neither of their parents had returned, they began to worry. Mum had never been gone this long and if she wasn't going to be home before they got back from school, she would leave a note to say where she was going and what time she would be back. There had been no note on the kitchen table.

Jamie had made some dinner for them both and tried to comfort Nicky, who was three years younger than him, by saying things like,

"Don't worry I'm sure they'll be home soon!" and, "I'm sure mum was just in a hurry and forgot to leave us a note." or "Dad probably has a meeting in town and he'll be home anytime now." But deep down Jamie was getting really worried, they had never ever been left so long on their own, their parents had told him many times that, at thirteen, he was still too young to be left in charge of Nicky.

He let Nicky watch some TV while he went to his room to listen to music but he kept looking at his alarm clock. He just couldn't understand why his parents hadn't called, it wasn't like them, he had wondered if they'd had an accident but then they weren't together so one of them should have come home by now! He didn't know what to do, he was the eldest, he *should* know what to do. By nine o'clock he'd decided to phone his best friend's mum. She had always treated Jamie like a second son.

When he told her what had happened she said not to worry, but he was to leave a note for his parents and to grab his and Nicky's night things and school stuff, she would be right over to get them.

But their parents didn't come home that night and the next morning they were sent off to school with a promise that, if Mrs.

Stirling heard anything, she would let the boys know straight away. But no word had come and by the time they got back to the Stirlings house the police were there, asking questions.

Now, one week later, they were standing on this windy platform, saying goodbye to the family that had taken them in, waiting to go and stay with an aunt they barely knew, in a place they had never heard of, for goodness knows how long!

Mrs. Stirling, a plain, mousy woman who looked very stern until she smiled, looked over at the two boys standing alone on the platform in the noisy train station and thought how different they were. Jamie, tall and thin with dark wavy hair and green eyes, had a way of making people like him, whilst Nicky, shorter and stockier with red, curly hair and dark brown eyes, was sensitive and much shyer, usually letting Jamie have the limelight but when you got to know him you realised, he had a comical side and would make you laugh even if you were angry at him.

Mrs Stirling and her husband, a tall man with a hunched back and a shock of black hair, walked over from the concession stand and gave the boys a couple of magazines and some sweets. Mrs Stirling smiled at them and said, dabbing the corner of her eyes,

"Your train's coming, now don't forget to write and let us know how things are, we'll miss you both very much". And she pulled them to her and gave them both a hug.

Smiling back, Jamie said "Thanks for everything and I promise we'll write as soon as we get there. Thanks for the magazines and sweets".

"Yeah thanks" Nicky mumbled, trying to show a brave face.

"Now hurry along boys" said Mr. Stirling jovially "You don't want to miss your train."

The train pulled into the station and the boys waved goodbye. Nicky climbed into an empty carriage followed by Jamie, they stowed their few belongings on the overhead racks and settled down beside the window for the long ride to the Cornwall coast.

The train moved slowly out of the station, picking up speed as it headed for the outskirts of London. The houses flashed past, soon they were in the countryside and the train didn't seem to be moving so fast, probably because the farms and buildings were further away. They could see the lights of cars on the distant roads as the unseen drivers hurried home to their families. Soon it would be getting too dark to see anything, it always got dark early this time of year, but for March it had been a beautiful sunny, if chilly, day, although Jamie hadn't noticed. All he could think about was; where were his parents? What had happened to them.... and what was going to happen to him and Nicky?

* * * *

By now it was pitch black outside and even though Jamie had been staring out of the window, he hadn't noticed the many stops the train had made.

He looked down at his watch and muttered, "Ten past nine, we should be there soon."

Nicky glanced up and looked quickly away but Jamie had noticed the tears in his eyes. He realised he hadn't even considered what Nicky must be going through. Nicky was so sensitive, he hated it when their parents quarrelled, it was usually because they couldn't agree how to punish *him* for hitting Nicky, Jamie thought regretfully.

Jamie smiled across at Nicky and said, "It's going to be okay. We should think of this as an adventure, we'll have loads to explore, mum says auntie lives on the coast. Just think of all the smugglers caves we can explore!"

"Yeah; that's great you'll either push me off a cliff or we'll be caught by smugglers!", Nicky replied, with a small smile on his face.

"But think about it, if we get caught sneaking onto their boat to see what they're smuggling, they'll tie us up in a cave... because the tide will be coming in and they want to dispose of any witnesses, we'll have to escape and of course we do, just as the water gets up to our necks.

"You forgot one important thing, you're a useless swimmer! I'll be okay 'cos I didn't chicken out of swimming lessons, I'll end up having to rescue you." Nicky replied grinning and ducking as Jamie chucked one of the magazines at him... which Nicky promptly chucked back.

They both had a good chuckle and before they realized it, the train was slowing down once again. Jamie lowered the window and stuck his head out, it was beginning to drizzle but he could clearly see the station sign, it read "EXETER".

He looked down at Nicky and said, "We're here".

Jamie reached up and handed down Nicky's bags and then grabbed his own. The train came to a halt and Nicky opened the door, stepped down onto the chilly, station platform, followed closely by Jamie.

"Can you remember what auntie looks like?" Nicky asked as they walked along the platform being jostled and bumped by the bustling crowd heading for the exit.

"Not really, I remember long, red hair but that's about it", Jamie answered, wondering if he would recognise his aunt "I guess we'll just wait for her to come to us, huh?"

Outside the station they stepped aside to allow the crowd to pass and looked around for their aunt. The station emptied, the taxis left with their fares and the boys were left alone in the chilly drizzle.

Jamie looked at Nicky and said "She'll be here soon, she probably got held up, let's wait inside,"

They were just turning around to head back inside when they heard a car approaching. They turned back. Coming down the road was an old Ford station-wagon, it looked like it would be more at home in America in the 50's than on these tiny country roads.

The station wagon pulled up in front of Jamie and Nicky and out jumped a short, plump woman with long, reddish-blonde hair that cascaded down her back to her waist. She ran over to the boys and engulfed them in a suffocating hug. When they had disentangled themselves from the folds of her flowing, dark green cloak, she looked from one to the other and gave a huge sigh and said,

"Oh my dears, I'm so glad you came, I've been so worried about you, but everything will be alright now." She smiled sympathetically at them and continued, "Look how you've grown, the last time I saw you two, you were just little tots." She swept an unruly lock of hair behind her ear "Shall we go? Throw your bags in the boot and jump in".

They did as they were told and very soon they were speeding along the dark, winding country lanes without a clue where they were or where they were going. Auntie Lydia kept up a dialogue of small talk until she ran out of things to say and then they continued in silence, broken only by the sound of the wipers squeaking on the windshield.

Jamie sat next to Nicky in the back seat looking out of the partially open window. It was very dark and there were no streetlights, they were bumped and tossed around for ages. Every now and then the cars headlights would fall on a signpost that Jamie managed to read, "Camelford", a little later another that said "Wadebridge". After what seemed to be ages of narrow, bumpy roads, the car slowed down and made a sharp left turn onto a dirt road. Travelling much slower, they wound their way along, the trees thicker now, sometimes the branches brushed the side of the station wagon, but still they kept going. Jamie could smell the salt air and began to wonder if they were lost.

Nicky whispered. "If we don't stop soon, we'll end up in the sea".

"That's just what I was thinking", Jamie whispered back.

Another turn and the station wagon emerged onto a wider country lane with fields on the right, neatly framed by a hedgerow. The car travelled for another minute or two before entering a small village called "Padstow Green". It looked like it had popped out of a storybook. The road circled the village green; a duck pond and a tall stone monument with a bronze plaque were in the middle of the green. On the other side of the green was a row of white, disjointed shops; first the Post Office, then the Hardware Shop, Greengrocers, Butchers, Newsagents and finally the Milliners. On the corner stood a stately Tudor building, bathed in a warm glow from the windows and the sign swaying gently in the breeze read "Witches Hat Inn". A faint sound of happy voices reached their ears as they passed.

They were now travelling along a narrow road with thatched cottages on either side, each with a small, neatly manicured garden. The station wagon slowed and seemed to struggle as it climbed a gently rising hill. Atop the hill, a tall, dilapidated wall came into view, large trees hung menacingly over it, their branches scraping the wall in the breeze like skeletal fingers scratching away at the plaster, to reveal the brick beneath. The station wagon slowed and turned as it passed through the wrought iron gates that hung precariously off their hinges. The driveway, which at one time must have been beautiful, was now overgrown. Rhododendron bushes twelve feet tall hung like a canopy over the driveway blocking out any light from the moon. The gravel beneath the wheels crunched as the station wagon moved slowly along the driveway then, looming out of the darkness, a monstrous wall of grey stone, three stories high, appeared.

Nicky instinctively reached out for Jamie, who turned and looked at the frightened expression on his face.

"Hey; it's an adventure, remember!" Jamie said smiling at him. Nicky tried to smile back but the knot in his stomach only made it look like a grimace. The station wagon came to a stop in front of the large weathered doors.

Auntie Lydia turned to face the boys and said kindly "I know it looks a bit gloomy but wait until you see it tomorrow, if it's a clear day you can see all the way to Wales". She jumped out to unlock the boot.

"A bit gloomy?" Nicky said.

"Well, it could be worse" Jamie said with a twinkle in his eye.

"No, it couldn't" Nicky answered.

"Yes it could, it could be thunder and lightning and Igor could open the door!" Jamie teased.

Nicky and Jamie retrieved their bags from the boot and followed Auntie Lydia. The front door suddenly flew open making Jamie and Nicky jump and, standing in the doorway, was a tall thin man with long, dark blonde hair tied back in a ponytail. His big brown eyes scrutinized the boys as he looked down his long straight nose and then the corners of his mouth turned up in a big smile. They smiled back, both of them assuming that this was their Uncle Morton.

He reached out, took their bags from them, and beckoned them to follow their Auntie, saying, "I'll take these up to your rooms".

The boys entered a large dimly lit front hall, a dank odour mingled with lemon polish hung in the air and a cold draft crept up their legs, making Nicky shiver. Jamie felt Nicky very close to him as they followed Auntie Lydia past the enormous staircase and through a door into a dark, narrow corridor, the only light came from a small wall sconce, which barely shed any light.

Auntie Lydia walked to the end of the corridor, with the boys close behind, and opened a door. Light flooded into the corridor, warm air touched their cold cheeks and the lingering aroma of fresh baked bread reached their noses. They entered a huge, old-fashioned kitchen with a red flagstone floor, whitewashed stone walls and ten foot high ceilings where massive, blackened beams spanned from wall to wall. Against the left wall, an ancient wood-burning stove stood, its blackened burners showing the years of use and in its belly, a fire crackled.

In the centre of the room was the largest wooden table the boys had ever seen, it could easily seat twenty people. Auntie Lydia had shed her cloak and was busy pouring milk into a saucepan, which she then placed on the stove, she reached up into the cupboard beside the stove and took out two cups. Placing them on the counter, she added cocoa and sugar.

She turned to see the boys still standing awkwardly in the doorway and smiled, indicating to two chairs and said, "Sit, sit!", then crossed the room and disappeared through another door, only to reappear a few seconds later with armfuls of food which she laid in front of them; a cold ham, cheese, fresh homemade bread, mince pies, biscuits, jam tarts, an apple pie! As if this wasn't enough, she then returned to the pantry appearing again with a big bowl of fresh fruit.

Jamie and Nicky suddenly realised that they were starving; they hadn't eaten anything since lunchtime, even though Mrs. Stirling had packed sandwiches for the trip, they hadn't felt much like eating, but now the aroma of homemade bread and apple pie made their mouths water. Soon the milk was boiling and Auntie Lydia poured it into the two cups and placed them in front of the boys, who eagerly picked them up and sipped the delicious hot chocolate. Auntie Lydia began to slice big wedges of bread for the boys, who hungrily ate everything she placed before them. They finished it all off with a large slice of apple pie and cold custard!

The boys sat back feeling warm, cosy and very full. Uncle Morton opened the door holding an oil lamp. "If you're ready I'll take you up to your rooms, so you can get settled", he said kindly.

They thanked their auntie and rose from the table feeling quite tired as they followed Uncle Morton back along the dark corridor and into the Front Hall. They slowly climbed the grand staircase; half way up, the stairs divided, leading off to the right and the left. Across the top of the right-hand stairs, hung a large tapestry, which was moving slightly from a breeze coming from somewhere behind it, a dank, mouldy smell seemed to be emanating from there too. Uncle Morton continued up the left-hand stairs and the boys followed, glancing back towards the other stairs as a shiver went down their spines. Uncle Morton, bathed in the light from the oil lamp, was the only thing the boys could see as he led them down the echoing hallway passing one door, then another and another. He turned at the end of the hallway and climbed a narrower set of stairs and along, yet another hallway.

Finally, Uncle Morton stopped beside a door, pointed to another at the end of the hallway and said, "That's the bathroom" and, reaching out for the door handle, he pushed open the door. A strange light flickered around the room, Uncle Morton walked in and the boys stood on the threshold looking around. A blazing fire in the ornately carved fireplace and candles burning in the wall sconces was causing the eerie shadows to dance around the room. The boys looked around and, as if reading their minds, Uncle Morton said,

"There's only electricity on the first floor and in the bathrooms, and we have running water too, so I'll have to show you how to use the emersion heater tomorrow." He said proudly.

Apprehensively, the boys stood on the threshold taking in the room; their uncle smiled and beckoned them in. The worn, dark floorboards creaked under their weight as they entered. The faded, blue velvet curtains at the windows matched the ones hanging around the four-poster bed; in front of the crackling fire were two overstuffed armchairs that looked like they could swallow anyone who sat in them. Between these was a small, shabby end table. Against the walls were various tables and dressers, all looking worse for wear, and on the floor was a very faded, threadbare rug.

Uncle Morton was opening a door in the far corner. He looked back at Jamie and said,

"And this is your room Jamie, we thought you might want to be right next door to your brother, the fire's lit and the bed's been aired".

The boys followed him into the other room, which was almost the same except narrower at one end; probably, thought Jamie, because the bathroom had been added at the end of the hallway. The curtains were red instead of blue. In front of the crackling fire stood an identical over-stuffed chair, beside this was a very worn, red leather armchair and between them stood an exquisite

Queen Anne table. Uncle Morton said, lighting the last oil lamp beside the bed,

"I'll say goodnight then, sleep tight and I'll see you in the morning." He walked over to the door to the hallway and quietly let himself out.

The boys walked over to the fireplace and Nicky fell into the overstuffed armchair and curled up, staring into the fire. Jamie sat in the other chair and looked at him. He looked so small in that chair, he felt like he had to protect him from the world, he wondered now, how he could have been so mean to Nicky just because he had wanted to tag along with him and his friends. He looked towards the fire. Both boys watched the flames playing leapfrog over the logs and thought about their parents.

Nicky and Jamie were left alone once again in strange surroundings, with only each other for comfort, as the raindrops hit the window panes and the wind whistled down the chimney. They sat watching the fire, feeling its warmth on their faces but feeling nothing but the coldness of pain inside, until sleep overcame them and they dragged their exhausted bodies to their beds.

Chapter Two

Charlotte's Diary

The next morning dawned sunny and bright. Nicky awoke from a peaceful dreamless sleep, stretched, rolled over and opened one eye. Recognition soon set in, he wasn't at home in his small, cramped bedroom that he always complained about, he was in this huge room in this huge house with people he didn't know. As he became aware of the familiar ache in his heart, he wished he could go back to sleep again.

He threw off his quilt and slid out of bed, walked over to the window, pulled back the heavy velvet curtains and looked out over, what he presumed used to be, the lawn but now looked more like a field, especially with the half dozen sheep grazing on it. A movement caught his eye. He glanced down at the low wall surrounding the veranda and there, stretching in the morning sun, was a grey, tabby cat. Nicky smiled and thought, "That's the life".

He turned from the window and noticed that his room was quite bright; he had thought last night, that it was very dark and dingy, but now he saw that it was spotlessly clean and Auntie had made an effort to make it comfortable for him. On one dresser were some photos of his mum and auntie's when they were young and on a table by the window was a vase of dried flowers. She had also thrown some hand-embroidered doilies onto other pieces of furniture to brighten up the dark wood. The walls were covered in light blue, silk wallpaper that seemed to have vines or something all over it.

He made his way over to the half open door that led into Jamie's room. They had agreed to leave the door open last night as neither one wanted to be completely on their own. Jamie was still sleeping; he looked tiny in the large four-poster bed. Nicky hopped up onto the bottom of the bed and waited for Jamie to wake up. Soon the chilly morning air crept over his body, the fire had gone out long ago and he hadn't put on his dressing gown so he grabbed up the bottom of the big, fluffy quilt and tried to wrap it around himself, but he pulled it off Jamie, who woke up and grumbled,

"Watcha doing? It's cold!".

"I know, that's why I want some quilt!", replied Nicky.

Angrily, Jamie said, "Well go back to your own room and leave my quilt alone!".

Realizing where he was and immediately regretting what he'd said he quickly added, "Never mind, jump in!"

And pulled out the covers so Nicky could crawl in beside him. Nicky clambered over the bed and fell in beside Jamie, who started laughing at Nicky's resemblance to a puppet without it's strings.

They lay there for awhile until Nicky said," You ought'a see the gardens, they look like fields and there's sheep too and it looks like they go all they way down to the sea!"

"The sheep go all the way down to the sea?" Jamie asked, confused.

"No, stupid! The lawn!" Nicky said, shaking his head.

"Well, why don't we go and explore?" said Jamie with a twinkle in his green eyes.

"And look for smugglers too, huh?" said Nicky, smiling.

Fifteen minutes later they were retracing their steps of last night. They hadn't seen much by the light of the oil lamp, but now they knew why it echoed so, there was absolutely no furniture or rugs, not even a painting in the hallway, it was completely bare.

The boys found their way down to the kitchen where a wonderful aroma met them. Auntie Lydia was busy preparing breakfast. Uncle Morton was sitting at the big wooden table reading a newspaper. When Jamie and Nicky came in, Auntie Lydia and Uncle Morton turned and smiled at them.

Auntie Lydia said, "Did you sleep well?" Both boys nodded and sat down at the table.

Uncle Morton looked over at them and asked, "What are you planning on doing today?"

Jamie replied, "We thought we'd go exploring, is the beach close?"

"Yes dear, if you cross the lawn to the woods and then just look for the Summer House, the steps down to the beach are right beside it but you must be very careful, the steps are a bit uneven and very steep," answered Auntie Lydia.

Nicky asked, "Why do you have sheep on the lawn?"

"They belong to one of the farmers, he lends them to me to help keep the grass down, I can't keep up with all the mowing", replied Uncle Morton.

"I can help, I cut our grass at home all the time!" Jamie said.

"Thanks, I'll probably take you up on that!"

The boys thanked their Aunt for a delicious breakfast of eggs, bacon, fried bread, fried tomatoes, toast and homemade strawberry jam before leaving the kitchen and running back upstairs to get their coats as it was still only March. It was bound to be cold and windy on the beach. They left by the front door and, as they walked around to the side of the house, they noticed that everything needed repair and maintenance. The garage, which was probably stables a century ago, was falling down. The twenty-foot brick wall that was obviously built as a windbreak was covered in ivy; the only thing that looked like it had been tended was the kitchen garden, with its neat rows of soil ready for planting and carefully pruned fruit trees.

Down the centre of the kitchen garden was a path that seemed to end at the brick wall and, as this was the only path the boys could see, they took it. After a few seconds of searching, Jamie found a latch, pressed down on it and put his weight against the door, which opened easily; much to Jamie's surprise and he stumbled through it. They were now standing at the edge of the "lawn" that Nicky had seen from his window; it looked even worse from down here.

The cold breeze brushed their cheeks and turned their noses red. They could smell the sea air as they walked through the long grass; following the slope of the lawn towards the woods at the far end. When they reached the trees they stopped and looked back towards the house. Even in daylight it looked spooky, with its bleak grey stones and round turrets on each corner. By counting the windows the boys realized that there were four floors to the turrets and only three to the rest of the house. One corner of the house looked like it was going to fall down, the turret on this corner had lost its pointed roof, along with half the wall on the fourth floor. Most of the windows were broken.

"I wonder if that's what's behind the tapestry?" asked Jamie, turning to Nicky, "We should explore that tomorrow, if we get the chance".

Inwardly, Nicky smiled at the twinkle in Jamie's eyes. And answered,

"Do you think they'll let us, it doesn't look very safe, it looks like it's about to fall down, I wonder what happened?"

"What they don't know, won't hurt them, I always say!" said Jamie, cockily.

The boys turned towards the woods looking for the Summer House. Not immediately seeing it, they began walking through the trees. Those on the outskirts were really nothing more than shrubs but as they went deeper they became taller and thicker, it was as if the woods were trying to reclaim the land. Just past an extremely old oak tree, which six people holding hands may just be able to encircle, they saw a building that, at one time, was probably very beautiful. It had eight sides and Gingerbread House style mouldings around the roofline. But now it was over-run with vines and bushes, very little paint remained on the plaster and the doors and windows were boarded up.

They fought their way through the undergrowth trying to peer between the boards to see inside, each window was shut up tight, except for one that was facing the sea; this board had been eroded by the weather and continuous sea winds and was hanging by one nail, its shutter hanging loose. Jamie pushed the shutter to one side and peered inside. The room was dark and musty, there were broken chairs and tables and leaves had blown through the window and covered the floor.

"Shall we see if we can get in?" asked Jamie.

Nicky nodded. Jamie grabbed hold of the loosest shutter and pulled, the screw in the hinge popped out easily and the shutter was left dangling to one side. Jamie reached in and unlatched the broken window, then hauled himself up and clambered in. Nicky quickly followed. After a few seconds their eyes adjusted to the dim light and they could see, against one wall, an old wicker couch. In front of this were a wicker table and a couple of wicker chairs. Against another wall, there was a broken table that looked like it had been hit with something very heavy, the legs had splayed out. There was a thick layer of dust on everything and cobwebs dangled down everywhere.

Nicky walked over to the couch and gingerly sat down. When it didn't break under his weight he relaxed and looked around. He was thinking that, with a bit of work, this would make a great clubhouse. He noticed some handwritten pieces of paper on the floor; they looked like they had been ripped out of a book. He called to Jamie as he reached for them,

"Come and look at this, this is really old, it looks like its from someone's diary!" Jamie walked over, sat down beside Nicky, and started to read.

"Dear diary,

Today was a bad day that horrible Mr. Smart came by and daddy made me visit with him, all I wanted to do was go to my secret place and read some more of Agatha's spell book, if I can learn one spell it would be to turn him into a toad."

Jamie bent down, picked up another piece, and started to read it.

"20ᵗʰ August, 1901

Dear Diary,

Daddy sent me to my room for being rude to Mr. Smart, he wants to marry me but he's ancient and I'm only 16, daddy said that the family needs Mr. Smart's money to keep the manor running, but why should I have to marry such a horrible person, why can't daddy find the money somewhere else. Agatha's spell book said that you can change pennies into guineas but I can only find half the book, if only I knew what happened to the other half I could turn all daddy's pennies into guineas and he wouldn't be so mad all the time."

"Wow! Who do you think wrote this and do you think she meant a real magic spell book?" asked Nicky excitedly.

Jamie shrugged his shoulders and said,

"I don't know, but one thing I do know, there's no such thing as magic, but it would be a good adventure to try and find out who wrote this and maybe find the rest of the diary".

"Where shall we start?" Nicky said grinning.

"How about right here, lets see if there's any loose panels, that would make a good, secret hiding place eh."

So both boys got up, walked over to opposite walls, and started tapping. They moved slowly around the room, tapping lightly every couple of inches, going up the wall then down; every time it sounded hollow, they stopped and tapped a little harder, then would look for a latch of some kind, but finding nothing, would move on.

After about fifteen minutes, they had gone around the whole room. They stopped and looked at each other.

"What about behind that painting over there?" Nicky asked.

Jamie walked over and lifted the large portrait of a young girl sitting under a tree, with the Summer House in the background. Jamie wiped the dust and cobwebs off and held it at arms length saying,

"That's this place and that tree she's sitting under must be that huge tree we passed"

Nicky walked over and stared at the picture then looked down at the bottom where a little brass plaque read, "Charlotte Whitehaven of Whitehaven Manor – 1899".

"I wonder if she wrote those notes. She would be about the right age." Nicky mused.

Jamie leant the portrait against the wall and tapped where it had hung. He noticed that one of the panels was loose. He reached into his pocket for his penknife, he pushed it between the panels, gave the hilt of the knife a tap with the palm of his hand, then tugged on the knife and the panel popped off.

Inside was a small cavity where four bricks had been removed and lying there covered in dust were two books. Jamie reached in and pulled them out. Written on the front was "Charlotte's Diary – 1900" and on the other was "Charlotte Whitehaven's Diary – 1899".

The boys walked over to the couch and sat down. Jamie handed Nicky the diary of 1899 and he started reading the other. He flicked through a couple of pages and then said,

"Listen to this! *"Dear Diary, It rained today, so I decided to go up to the north tower, I know daddy told me not to, but I had to get away from Mrs. Crabb the housekeeper, she is always telling me about her dear brother and how he made a fortune in Africa, I have heard the stories so many times I could not stand to hear them again. I sneaked up the stairs to the north tower and I went right up to the top, at the top of the stairs there was a door and it was locked but I knew where daddy kept a bunch of keys in his bedchamber so I went to find them. I unlocked the door; you wouldn't believe what I found. It had been someone's bedchamber at some time. There was a bed and a dresser and a big wardrobe, when I opened it I found all these old fashioned dresses, BUT hidden at the back under a suitcase I found a very old book, actually half a book, on the cover it read, Agatha's Spell Book. I took it, locked the door, and quickly went back down. I had to find somewhere to hide it before daddy caught me with it. But I'm not going to tell you in case someone finds and reads you."*

Jamie looked up and said, "Well wha'dya think?"

Nicky didn't say anything, so Jamie continued, "Do you think that room's still there, maybe we should see if we can find it?"

"Let's read some more first, see if we can find some more clues to Agatha's Spell Book". Nicky replied.

They continued to read, but it was more of the same thing. Nicky's diary, being a year earlier, was more about riding lessons and birthday parties. After about ten minutes, they decided there wasn't going to be anything useful in the earlier diary and put it to one side.

Jamie looked at his watch and said. "Auntie'll be expecting us for lunch soon, we'd better put these back and come back tomorrow."

So they returned the diaries to their hiding place, rehung the portrait and climbed back through the window. Jamie relocked the broken window and pushed the hinge screws back into their holes. He stood back and said. "No-one 'll know anyone's been inside."

As they walked back across the lawn to the Manor, Nicky said. "D'ya think we could borrow some stuff to clean it up a bit?"

"I don't think we should ask Auntie, she might say it's too dangerous to be inside there, but we could look around for some cleaning stuff, a house that size must have more than one broom." replied Jamie.

They retraced their steps through the gate in the wall just as Uncle Morton came out of the kitchen door. "I was just coming to look for you two, lunch is on the table, did you have fun on the beach?

Jamie gave Nicky a "Don't say anything" look and answered, "Yeah".

They had reached the back door and the most delicious smell met them. "Your aunt has gone all out for your first real meal with us so I hope you're hungry." Uncle Morton said smiling.

"Yeah, I'm starving", they answered together.

The smell of roast pork mingled with applesauce and fresh baked bread made their mouths water, but what a sight met their eyes; the wooden table had four place settings and almost every inch of the rest of the table was covered with food! Beside the enormous roast pork, applesauce and fresh bread, there was a bowl of roast potatoes, steamed carrots, Yorkshire puddings, a salad, a platter of fresh vegetables, homemade strawberry jam, a basket of fresh fruit, also the leftover apple pie and a big jug of piping hot custard.

The boys walked over to the kitchen sink and washed their hands under the icy cold water. On the stove a big kettle was singing. Jamie looked at his aunt and said,

"We don't usually get this much food for lunch, especially on a Friday, Mum usually goes all out on Sun..day ....." his voice trailed off and he looked at Nicky who was looking sadly back at him. They both had the same thought, "Where were Mum and Dad".

Auntie Lydia quickly covered the silence by hustling them over to the table and sitting them down, chattering as she did so. She and Uncle Morton sat down opposite the boys and started handing them plates of food. The boys began to eat and the sad thoughts soon faded.

When their plates were nearly empty, Auntie Lydia said,

"I thought we would take a walk down to the village tomorrow, so you can have a look around, you can by a postcard from the post office and mail it to those nice people who looked after you."

"You might want to show them the village school as well, as they will be going there on Monday?" Uncle Morton mused.

The boys looked up from their plates, mouths open, shocked expressions on their faces. They hadn't even thought about school, only about leaving their school friends behind. Auntie Lydia saw the shocked expressions and gave Uncle Morton a scornful look, and said,

"Well dears you do have to keep up your education and we don't really know how long you'll be staying do we? If you like we can go at the end of school today and I can introduce you to your teachers, it's a very small school and there are only two teachers, there aren't a lot of children in the village."

The boys agreed that it would be a good idea to meet the teachers before Monday. So after they had finished eating and helping Auntie Lydia with the dishes, they had just enough time to explore the first floor of the house. Auntie Lydia said she would just pop upstairs to change and then they would be off.

The boys left the warmth of the kitchen and went back to the chilly Front Hall to look around. The Front Hall was a lot brighter than they originally had thought, due to the large windows high above the front door opposite the grand staircase. Except for the door leading to the kitchen, there were only two other doors visible in the Front Hall, one on the right and one on the left. They opened a door to the right of the stairs, it was the Morning Room, this room faced east and was bright and cheery with yellow, floral curtains at the bay windows in the alcove, the window seats had the same faded fabric on the cushions. There were all different sizes of chairs and tables scattered around the room, but it was warm and cosy and smelled of lemon furniture polish.

They closed the door, crossed the hall and opened another door. This was the Library, it smelled of musty old books, which wasn't surprising as each side of the fireplace had floor to ceiling bookcases filled with old books. There were two dark-green, leather armchairs placed in front of the fireplace. Between these was a small oak table with a couple of books and a lamp on it. In the alcove sat an enormous, dusty mahogany desk with a worn, leather chair pushed back against the window. The surface of the desk was littered with envelopes and pieces of paper, but their eyes were fixed on the portrait over the fireplace. A man in his 30's with dark slicked down hair stared down at them with black unfeeling eyes. A pencil- thin moustache and the slight curl to his mouth made it look as if he was sneering. They walked over to the portrait and read the brass plaque at the bottom, it said "Jeremy Whitehaven – 1886".

Nicky said, "D'ya think that's Charlotte's dad, he looks mean enough, dunn'e?"

Jamie answered, "We could always ask, but then they might ask how we know about Charlotte?"

They left the Library, closing the door behind them, and walked to the left of the grand staircase, into the Portrait Gallery. The only light coming into this room was through the huge French Doors spanning the whole of the back wall of the Gallery. These doors led into the Conservatory, which was at the back of the house. Hundreds of portraits hung on the remaining three walls, some dating back 400 or 500 years.

The boys spotted a painting of a small, pretty woman with reddish- blonde hair and green eyes sitting under the same oak tree as Charlotte was in her portrait. The plaque read, "Margaret Whitehaven – 1884" and, the more they looked at it, the more they realised that she looked a lot like Charlotte or maybe Charlotte looked a lot like her, this was obviously Charlotte's mother.

"You noticed? A lot of the paintings have the same last name and it isn't Whitehaven, it's Padstow" Jamie asked

"Yeah, the really old ones, some look like they've bin' in a fire."

One painting caught Nicky's eye. "See this one, it's Agatha Ballystock!"

Jamie came over to look; she looked similar to Margaret, with the same reddish- blonde hair and green eyes, but she had a kind of wild look about her, like a caged animal. She couldn't have been much more than fifteen or sixteen.

"Do'ya think she's the same Agatha who wrote the spell book... if it really exists, of course?" Jamie said, correcting himself.

The boys were just looking at the portrait of a couple who looked like they were Margaret and Agatha's parents when they heard Auntie Lydia calling from the Front Hall. They hurried into the hall to find her standing by the open door wrapped in a shabby green shawl over a long, flowing skirt, carrying a straw bag. They grabbed their coats and followed Aunt Lydia out of the front door.

Instead of walking up the driveway to the main gate, they went left and followed the narrow gravel service road that divided the unkempt front lawns from the equally unkempt pasture.

"You will probably want to take this road to school as it's a lot quicker," Lydia said, reaching out to pull open the wrought iron gate to the street. "Morton can walk with you on Monday, on his way to work".

"He works?" Nicky said surprised.

"Yes dear, your uncle is the butcher, that's how come we have such nice meat," she said with a twinkle in her bright green eyes. "He takes the left fork into the village," she pointed down the hill, "the school's down that way," she pointed to the right, "and when you come home for lunch, you can go straight around to the side of the house to the kitchen door, we rarely use the front door anymore", she said cheerfully as they crossed the road. "Down there's the newer cottages as well, the ones in the village are much older, these are only about a hundred years old."

The boys looked where she was pointing but could only see a little bit of the end cottage as a large hedge blocked their view. Watching them from under the hedge was the grey tabby-cat.

Nicky asked, "If those are a hundred years old, how old are the ones in the village?"

"The oldest one is about 600 years old, but most of the original homes were replaced about 400 years ago, after the big fire destroyed the village." she replied, "The graveyard is even older than that, you should check out all the gravestones and see some of the dates".

By this time they had reached the fork in the road; they took the right fork and within a few minutes the village school came into view. It was a small, two-storey red brick building surrounded by a wrought iron fence atop a three-foot high brick wall. Above the double doors, written in the concrete in large letters was 'Built in 1951".

As they reached the gate, the door to the school opened and out came a small, round man with a salt and pepper goatee, wearing traditional teachers' robes. He saw Lydia entering the gate and gushed forward, hands held out saying, "Mrs. Ainsley, how nice to see you, I heard you were having visitors, are these your nephews from London?"

Lydia smiled politely and replied, "Hello Mr. Pennith, yes this is Jamie, he's thirteen and this is Nicky, he's ten and they're hoping to join you on Monday if that's alright. They could be staying with us for awhile".

"Of course, of course, that's not a problem at all, come in and have a look around, Mrs. Pennith is marking books in her classroom, but I'm sure she won't mind the interruption."

They followed him into the school. It was divided in half by a wide corridor down the centre; on the walls forgotten coats and bags hung from pegs and the odd Wellington boot stood in shoe racks under each peg. At the end was a staircase leading to the second floor and just before the staircase, opposite each other, were the classroom doors.

Mr. Pennith beckoned them through an open door. Sitting at a large desk, with two piles of exercise books obscuring her view, was a small woman with grey hair pulled tightly back in a neat little bun. She looked towards the door, her glasses balancing precariously on the end of her nose, she rose from her desk, removing her glasses as she did so and walked towards Lydia.

"Lydia how nice to see you, I was just saying, wasn't I dear? That I should call you so you could bring your nephews around so they could have a look at our little school, I'm sure it's nothing like their big London schools, but we like it, don't we dear?"

Jamie noticed her voice sounded a little too sweet as if she was trying very hard to be polite, he also noticed his aunt stiffen and the smile on her face seemed to be frozen there.

"Well, let's have a look at these boys," Mrs. Pennith continued, turning a false smile on the boys. "Well! You don't look much like Padstows do you? Maybe your eyes" she said to Jamie, "and your hair" as she turned her gaze on Nicky.

"Why should we?" Nicky asked curiously.

Mrs. Pennith's eyebrows raised and she looked at Lydia in surprise. Lydia responded "My sisters and I are descendants of the Padstow family, but there hasn't been a Padstow around for hundreds of years."

"Why?" asked Nicky again.

"That's a long story and I'll have to tell you another time, right now why don't you look around so I can talk to your teachers".

The boys walked off and surveyed their surroundings; the pupils' desks were set out in four neat rows facing the teachers desk, behind which was a large blackboard; at the back of the classroom was a long wall to wall counter and on this counter were piles of text books, exercise books, sketch pads, pens, pencils and crayons, all neatly laid out. Above the counter was a bank of high windows. They were obviously only for letting in light as they were way too high to see out of and the only way to open them was with a long pole. On one wall were posters of the times-tables from one to twelve and on the opposite wall were paintings the pupils had done.

"Boys!" Lydia called and the boys walked over to her. "Mr. Pennith will be your teacher Jamie and you, Nicky, will be with the younger children in Mrs. Pennith's class."

"I'll walk you out," said Mrs. Pennith.

The boys said goodbye to Mr Pennith and headed for the main door behind their aunt and Mrs. Pennith. At the school gate, as the adults were talking, Jamie touched Nicky's arm, put his hand up to his mouth and whispered, "Did you notice Mrs. Pennith's ring? It's the same as Auntie's".

Nicky looked at their fingers and sure enough the rings were the same. The ring had a black stone, set into that was a gold "C" entwined around a green "P". He whispered back, "What do you think it stands for and why does the teacher have the same ring as Auntie?"

Chapter Three

The Padstows

Saturday morning arrived with a bang. Big black clouds hung heavily in the sky as thunder crashed and lightning lit up the dark rooms of the mansion. A wall of water fell from the sky and soaked everything and anything silly enough to be out in it.

The smell of bacon wafted up the grand staircase and mingled with the odour of dank stones. Nicky was just heading down the draughty hallway to the grand staircase when Jamie ran up behind him.

"We can't go outside today so lets search the North Tower."

"Okay" Nicky replied as they both skipped down the stairs, two at a time.

Entering the cosy, warm kitchen, Auntie Lydia looked up from the stove and wished them a good morning. Jamie asked if they could help, but she said everything was done and produced a big platter of eggs and bacon, with another full of toast then she went into the pantry and came out with two pots of homemade jam.

"You don't have to cook all this for us, we're used to cereal and juice in the morning." Jamie said

"Well maybe during the week when you have to get to school you can have cereal and toast, I'd better put that on my shopping list," she said, looking around for the pen and pad, "I'm going into the village later to do some shopping, you can stay here if you want, it's not a nice day to look around the village".

"Okay" said the boys, tucking into the delicious food.

This works out great; Uncle Morton was at the butcher's shop and Auntie Lydia was going into the village, that would give them plenty of time to explore behind the tapestry. Jamie thought grabbing another slice of thick toast and slopping on strawberry jam.

"We'll do the dishes, if you want to get ready." Jamie said after breakfast.

"Thank you, that will be very helpful." Auntie Lydia said, taking off her apron and laying it on the back of a chair before going upstairs to get changed.

"Why'd you say we'd do the dishes, I hate doing dishes!" Nicky said crossly.

"Because the sooner she leaves the sooner we can go exploring" Jamie answered smiling. So Nicky grabbed the tea towel and started drying the dishes.

A few minutes later Auntie Lydia reappeared, she had tied back her long hair and put on a sweater. She smiled at the boys as she reached for a raincoat from behind the kitchen door.

"I should be about an hour, will you be alright by yourselves?" she asked as she put on some Wellington boots and a plastic rain hat,

"Yes, we'll be fine, I'm sure there's plenty to keep us busy in a house this size," Jamie said innocently.

"Well okay then, but stay in the house, I don't want you wandering around the estate in this weather." She picked up her straw basket and the shopping list, "Goodbye then, see you shortly." and walked out the kitchen door.

The boys quickly finished the dishes and, before rushing out, grabbed an oil lamp from the pantry. Their footfalls echoed through the empty house as they ran up the old staircase. They stopped in front of the tapestry and Jamie pushed it aside. It was damp to the touch and very heavy. They slipped behind it; Jamie lit the lamp and found that the hallway was the same as on the other side, long dark and empty. The two doors immediately to the right of the stairs and facing the front of the mansion were the bathroom and the East Turret Room; to the left of the stairs was the hallway with one door on the left side and two on the right.

Jamie tried the handle of the first door, it was stiff but it opened. Nicky was trying the one on the other side of the hallway but it was locked. He turned back when he heard Jamie open the door. The room hadn't been entered for years, everything was covered in dustsheets, a thick layer of dust was on everything and cobwebs hung in a mass of silvery threads. The boys shivered, the cold draft and dank smell were obviously coming from this side of the house. Jamie closed the door.

At the end of the hallway, opposite the stairs to the third floor, was another door, they turned the tarnished brass doorknob and the heavy door creaked open. This was the North Turret Room they had seen from the woods. The room was empty apart from the thick carpet of dust on the floor and the rain splashing in through the broken windows. They closed the door and climbed the stairs to the next floor.

Nicky opened the door to the third floor Turret and found an outer room with a spiral staircase and a door to the inner Turret Room; they walked over to the heavy oak door, placed the lamp on the floor and tried to push it open, it took both of their strengths to get it open enough for them to squeeze through. A few of the stones at the top of the wall had fallen in and daylight was peaking through, and part of the ceiling had collapsed. They squeezed back through the door, picked up the lamp and headed up the spiral staircase. They could feel the rain in the breeze as it came down the stairs and could smell the sea air, both the handrail and steps were slippery, so they had to tread carefully. Then the flame in the lamp flickered and went out.

The boys reached the top of the stairs by the dim grey light coming from above. Their mouths dropped open, the devastation they found was shocking; the heavy oak door was lying against the stair's handrail, half the turret wall was missing, the roof had collapsed into the room and the rain was pouring in, soaking everything. Jamie put the lamp on the ground again. Gingerly, they stepped inside the room; they could see the remnants of a bed and table under the collapsed roof. Against the farthest wall away from the damage stood an old weathered wardrobe, Jamie slid along the wall then crawled under a roof beam leaning against the wall and opened the wardrobe door; there was a loud hiss and something hit Jamie's chest, knocking him backwards, Nicky screamed with fright and both boys turned to see the tail of a grey tabby-cat disappearing down the staircase.

"How'd that get in there?" Jamie asked, rubbing his chest and panting hard.

Nicky stood pressed against the door jam with his hand over his heart, his mouth wide open and his brown eyes the size of saucers. Jamie soon recovered and started laughing

"You ought to see your face!" Jamie said, laughing harder

"You can talk!" Nicky said, laughing too.

They stood laughing at each other, and wiping tears from their eyes. Shortly the laughter subsided and Jamie peered inside the wardrobe; he saw old-fashioned dresses but no books or anything else that might say who the clothes belonged to.

"This's got to be the room Charlotte wrote about, huh?" Nicky asked.

"Yeah, but I'd love to know how it was destroyed, it looks like a bomb went off! Jamie replied, making his way back along the wall to the door.

"Maybe Agatha's spell?" Nicky answered.

"Yeah right!" Jamie scoffed.

They walked down the dimly lit hallway of the third floor, trying the doors to see if any opened. On the second try a door opened, Jamie looked at Nicky with a smile and the door squeaked as he pushed it open for them to step inside. The room was like the others, dust and cobwebs everywhere, big heavy curtains, covered in dust, hanging at the windows and around the bed, but unlike the other rooms, not everything was covered with dustcovers. Some dustcovers lay on the floor. This room appeared to be a child's room, there was a rocking horse by the window and some dolls sat on the dresser.

Nicky walked over to the fireplace where he absentmindedly began touching the knick-knacks on the mantelpiece. When the ornate carvings of acorns underneath the mantelpiece caught his eye, he ran his fingers over them, but stopped on one that protruded more than the others; he gave it a slight push and heard a scraping noise. He looked over to the left side of the fireplace; part of the panelling on the mantelpiece was sticking out! He reached over and pulled it open, it was a secret drawer.

"Hey Jamie, come look at this!" Nicky called, staring down at the drawer.

What they found surprised them both; there lay Agatha's Spell Book. Jamie reached in and carefully pulled it out. He stepped back, placed the book on the table beside the armchair, and opened it. The pages were faded and brittle, but in fancy writing they could just make out titles like "*Egg Laying Spell*" and "*Milk Producing Spell*" and "*A Potion to Mend Broken Bones*". Together they read the spells, one after the other, some so faded or ripped that they could make out only half of it.

"Can we try one?" Nicky asked.

"I doubt if they'll work, I keep telling you there's no such thing as magic," Jamie said. "But we gotta go, where d'ya think we should hide it, here, or our rooms, or maybe in the Summer House?"

"I dunno, if we leave it here it will be safe, but we won't be able to get at it whenever we want to: if we leave it in our room, Auntie might find it when she's cleaning, and the Summer House is too far away from the house!" Nicky replied.

"Well, let's leave it here for now, and we can look and see if we have a secret hiding place in our rooms." said Jamie

"Yeah, sounds good!" Nicky responded.

Jamie placed the book back in its hiding place, had a quick look around for anything else and then beckoned Nicky to follow him out. He closed the door and they headed back to the grand staircase.

Jamie looked at his watch again, "We'd better hurry she's been gone for over an hour".

They quickened their steps and had just reached the tapestry, when they heard Auntie Lydia calling from the kitchen. They slipped out from behind the tapestry and ran down the stairs and through to the kitchen, where they found a very wet and wind-swept Auntie unpacking a couple of bags of groceries.

"I'll help!" Nicky said, helping her put the groceries in the pantry.

"I'll put the kettle on for tea, shall I?" Jamie asked, walking over and filling the kettle with water. She thanked the boys as she sat at the table, drying the ends of her long ponytail.

"This is very nice, I haven't had anyone make me tea for ages", she said smiling.

"We always help mum put the groceries away and make her tea too," Nicky said, feeling the now-familiar ache in his heart.

"Well don't you worry, we'll hear from her soon, I know we will!" Auntie replied hopefully. Brightening up she asked "So, what have your two been doing while I was gone, exploring no doubt?"

They blushed a little and Jamie said. "Well yeah, we saw the damage on the other side of the house when we went to the beach and we thought we would get a closer look".

"That's very dangerous in the north wing, you really should stay on this side; promise me you will dears?"

"Yes Auntie", Nicky said.

"Okay, but how did it get damaged"

Auntie Lydia rose and walked over to the pantry as she replied, "Lightning, many, many years ago, before I was borne," she reappeared with a tin of biscuits, "I like biscuits with my tea, don't you?"

Feeling like she had purposefully changed the subject, Jamie casually asked, "Is there a family tree of the Padstows, we were looking at the portraits and we would like to know who's who?"

"Well I'm sure there is, dear, but I don't know where it is, it will probably be in the library in one of the books; why don't you go and have a look while I make some lunch."

"Great, come on Nick!" Jamie eagerly replied.

The boys left the kitchen and went to the library. They stood staring at the wall of books not knowing where to start.

Jamie said, "You start this side and I'll start over there", and he walked over to the far side of the fireplace "It will probably be a fairly big book, going by how many paintings are in the gallery".

Nicky nodded and started at one corner and worked his way across. Jamie climbed up the wooden ladder that was attached to the bookshelves and started to check some large books on the top shelf. After about half an hour Auntie Lydia came in and said, "Any luck?"

"No!" Nicky said, plopping down in one of the armchairs in front of the fireplace.

"Well never mind, your uncle will be home at half past twelve, then you can ask him if he's seen one, he's been through all the books, he was cataloguing them for my father, that's how I got to know him," she said with a roguish smile "My sister Amy was interested in him too, but he chose me."

"What about Mum, was she interested in anyone in the village?" asked Jamie.

"Not seriously, your mum was more interested in going to college, she wanted to be an architect; I guess this old place got to her, she always wanted to rebuild the north wing ever since she was little, but then she met your dad at college and well... I guess.. they decided to have a family instead," she said in a melancholy tone.

"Why hasn't anyone fixed it?" Nicky asked.

"Money mostly, we may live in a mansion but we don't have any money!" she answered.

"Why don't you leave then?" Jamie asked.

"Leave!! We couldn't do that; this is our home, where would we go? No, there has always been a Padstow here, even if we don't have the name anymore, we're still Padstows", she answered, her voice rising slightly. She abruptly turned and walked out of the room.

"Wow! What was all that about?" Jamie asked.

"I guess you upset her." Nicky answered, thinking that Jamie could be insensitive at times.

At half past twelve Nicky was setting the table while Jamie placed dishes of hot food in the centre when a rather wet Uncle Morton walked through the back door. He wiped his feet and hung up his soaked raincoat on the hook beside the door. Auntie Lydia looked up and smiled at him, he crossed the room and kissed her tenderly on the cheek.

"Had a nice morning?"

"Well the boys have been looking for the family tree in the library but can't find it".

"I think I saw it on the top shelf, it's a big thick book, with a red cover." Uncle Morton answered.

After lunch Uncle Morton said goodbye and returned to the shop, Auntie Lydia told the boys to go and have fun looking for the book, and she went about cleaning up the kitchen. The boys ran off to the library and Jamie climbed the ladder again to continue the search of all the red-covered books. Within a few minutes he pulled down a promising looking book, he opened it up.

"Got it" he exclaimed, climbing back down. "This is going to be harder than I thought, it's not a chart, it's just a list of names, lets see if we can match them up to the paintings."

So the boys left the library and crossed the Front Hall to the Portrait Gallery.

"Let's start with the last name in the book and work backwards." suggested Nicky.

"Good idea, not counting Mum and our aunties, that would be Daisy Talbot … is she here?" Jamie asked, looking around.

"Yeah, she's over here" Nicky said from the far corner. Jamie walked over and looked up at the portrait, "She was married to Marvin Disbury. Next is Rosemary Talbot, yeah that's her right beside Daisy, no husband. Okay, how about Primrose Whitaker?"

"Yeah she's here next to Edward Talbot" Nicky answered.

"That's her husband, so these two are the parents of Daisy and Primrose", pointed Jamie. "Okay, what about Penelope Pickerall married to Arnold Whitaker, that makes them parents to Primrose Whitaker. Charlotte's name is here, she was born 1885, but there's no husband beside her name, I guess she didn't get married after all".

"Here's Penelope next to Patricia Pickerall" Nicky said.

"Okay, Patricia was born 1882; she was married to James Ainsley. He must be related to Uncle Morton" Jamie answered "How about Emily Ballystock married to Robert Pickerall?"

"Right above them, next to Margaret Ballystock and Agatha Ballystock, Margaret must be Charlotte's mum before she was married!" Nicky said excitedly, "Look at this, all the older portraits say Padstow Mansion, then here it changes to Whitehaven Manor". Jamie looked then shrugged his shoulders.

"It says here Margaret was born in 1860, Agatha was born 1859 and Emily was born 1864, which makes Agatha the oldest, so how come Margaret and Jeremy Whitehaven got the house, doesn't it usually go to the oldest child?"

"And what gives him the right to change the name to Whitehaven Manor" Nicky said indignantly.

"This is interesting" said Jamie with his head cocked sideward trying to read something scribbled down the side of the page, "It says…. "Nothing good can come from Margaret marrying an outsider the risk is too great even if the curse is broken"

"Wonder what they mean?" asked Nicky curiously. Jamie shrugged again.

"Okay, who's next?" asked Nicky.

Prudence Pennith – 1838 married Harold Ballystock, our teachers must be related to her".

"Here they are," Nicky said "that makes them the parents of Agatha, Margaret and Emily"

"Sophie Pennith married Charles Boyd and Annie Pennith married Harold Pendoggett, their parents are Emily Berwick and William Pennith.

"They're over here." Nicky said, walking to the other end of the wall.

"I guess it's true what Auntie said, there's been no males born for hundreds of years, going through this book." Jamie said flipping through the pages "the last male Padstow was Godfrey Padstow, son of Simon Padstow, are they here?"

"Simon is here, he looks like he's been in a fire, his edges are scorched, and here's Godfrey", Nicky replied, walking to the opposite wall where the oldest paintings were hung.

The boys continued going around the room, checking the book and matching the names with the portraits, for another hour. When they had finished, they went looking for Auntie Lydia. They found her in the Morning Room cleaning out the grate, she looked up as they entered and asked, "How goes the search?"

"Well, we found the book and tried to match the names with the portraits; there's a couple missing, but we're curious; how come Jeremy Whitehaven changed the name of the Mansion?"

"Ah, that's easy to explain, he was a very arrogant man and bought himself into the family, the Pickeralls were having money problems like all the families before them and he thought he could buy his way in, so when Margaret inherited, he changed the name from Padstow Mansion to Whitehaven Manor and no-one ever bothered to change it back. Mind, most of the villagers, past and present, refer to it as "The Mansion", so it really doesn't matter."

"Why don't you change it back?" asked Nicky.

"Never really thought about it, I would have to consult my sisters first, we inherited the estate equally you see."

"So how come you and Uncle live here alone?" asked Nicky.

"Your Auntie Amy lives here but she likes travelling abroad, but when she's in England, she comes home." she replied.

"So mum grew up in this house?" Jamie asked.

"Yes, we all did, even though we didn't have much money, we had a lot of fun here exploring the Mansion and the grounds, playing Hide N' Seek on rainy days, didn't your mum ever tell you about her childhood?" Lydia asked curiously.

"No, she never tells us anything, when we ask she only ever tells us stories about being in college and meeting Dad", Jamie answered.

"How come there's no paintings of you lot?" Nicked asked.

"Our parents couldn't afford to have them done, your grandmother is there though."

"Which one?" Nicky said excitedly.

"Daisy Talbot. She married Marvin Disbury, but there's no painting of him either." Lydia said. Nicky ran off to check it out.

Jamie decided to ask another question. "What happened to Charlotte Whitehaven? She didn't get married so the books says".

"I don't know dear, why don't you check out the graveyard tomorrow, there's not much to do on Sundays. Uncle Morton will be doing some gardening and I'll be tidying up Amy's rooms, she should be back soon." Lydia said.

"Okay, if you don't think Uncle Morton will want any help." he said happily.

"No dear, you go and have some fun while you can, on Monday you'll have to settle down to school work, so enjoy your last day of freedom!" she replied with a grin.

Jamie smiled back and looked out of the window. The sun was peeking out behind a fluffy white cloud and the rain had stopped.

"I think we'll take a wander down to the village post office, it looks like the sun's coming out." he said. Auntie Lydia nodded and went back to her cleaning.

Jamie found Nicky in the conservatory looking up through the glass roof.

"That's my room up there, I saw this roof when I looked out the window this morning." Nicky commented.

The conservatory was a big, square room built between the two wings of the house, it backed onto the Portrait Gallery. French doors led into the study on the left and the dining room on the right, two sets of French doors led out to the veranda and above was a glass roof that really needed to be cleaned. A few pieces of wicker furniture were placed around the room haphazardly, in the centre was a large, round raised flowerbed, which probably had a tree of some sort in it originally, but now there was just bare soil.

"I thought we'd go to the village as the sun's coming out and send a postcard, whatcha think?" Jamie asked.

"Yeah sure!" Nicky answered.

The boys went to fetch their coats and yelled goodbye to their Aunt as they left the house. The air smelled fresh and clean after the storm and the birds were singing in the drenched trees. On the hill, a lady with a couple of small children was coming up from the village, she looked at the boys, grabbed her childrens' hands and crossed to the other side of the road, she then acted like the boys weren't even there. Jamie looked at Nicky and Nicky shrugged his shoulders. They reached the village in about fifteen minutes, there were a number of people entering and leaving the shops, some were talking together on the pavement but as Nicky and Jamie approached, they stopped talking, looked at Nicky and Jamie and started whispering behind their hands, then quickly walked away.

"Is it my imagination or are these people acting weird?", asked Jamie. Nicky nodded.

The boys found the Post Office at the end of the street and entered. Inside was a stout middle-aged lady behind the cage, talking to an elderly man; they both turned as the bell rang above the door. The lady involuntarily stepped back and the elderly man gave them a strange look, mumbled, "I'll talk to you later!" and left.

The boys walked over to the rack with the postcards, strangely there were no picture postcards, only plain white ones!. Jamie picked one up and went over to another rack, found a writing pad and some envelopes among the birthday cards and stationary and said,

"I'll buy these too, so we can write to our mates".

Jamie walked to the counter. The lady hadn't taken her eyes off the boys since they walked in, she gave her head a little shake as he approached, smiled nervously and moved forward.

"So you're Lydia's nephews are you?" She said, trying to sound casual, "Come for a short visit I hear, I hope you enjoy your stay, that's £3.25p". She placed the items in a paper bag and handed it through the slot as Jamie slid £4 through; she gave him his change, he thanked her and they left.

"Now I'm sure these people are weird, did you see the way she backed away from us?" Jamie said, once they were back outside.

"Yeah and the old guy, the way he ran out as soon as we came in, it was like we had the plague or sum'ut!" Nicky said.

"Do you want to freak out the person in the hardware shop?" Jamie grinned, as he reached for the doorknob of Pickeralls Hardware Shop.

The shop was a lot bigger than the Post Office, but dimly lit, the window was so full of tools and such that very little light came through. Shelves from floor to ceiling lined the walls and there were two long tables down the centre packed with everything imaginable. Boxes labelled "mixing bowls" sat on the floor with a set of mixing bowls balanced precariously on top. Leaning against the counter were brooms, dust mops and floor mops of all shapes and colours. Lining the front counter were bins full of nails, screws, nut and bolts.

The boys began to browse through the shelves picking things up, making little comments to each other, and then putting the item back. Nicky picked up a penknife and was opening up all it's features, when a voice behind him made him jump.

"Are you going to buy that or just play with it?"

Nicky turned to find a stocky man with bulging blue eyes staring at him, his arms crossed in front of his large stomach.

"I was thinking about it, how much is it?" Nicked asked politely.

"£5 to you!" he replied crossly.

"How much to a villager?" Jamie asked sweetly, walking up beside Nicky.

The shopkeeper cast Jamie a dirty look. "The same!" he replied.

"You can get one for half that in London, Nick, don't waste your money!" Jamie said and steered Nicky to the shelf he'd been looking at. The shopkeeper went back to the counter to ring in a sale. But he kept one eye on the boys.

"See what I see?" whispered Jamie.

Nicky looked and right in front of them were jars of things with strange names like "Eye of Newt", "Dragons' Blood", "Crows' Feet" and "Wolf's Bane", there were also packages of hemlock, "Elf's Dust", "Ground Bat's Wing" and liverwort. Nicky noticed the shopkeeper coming out from behind the counter so he elbowed Jamie. The boys moved along the shelves. In the next section there were books with titles like, "The Guide to Proper Potion Making" by Prudicia Austell, "How To Become a Powerful Sorcerer" by Dragos Pendoggett and "The Only Spell Book You Will Ever Need" by Pugnacious Boyd. On another shelf were sparkly rocks of all shapes and sizes with names like "Rose Quartz", "Turine" and "Citrine".

The shopkeeper, his eyes bulging even more, came forcefully towards them.

"No browsing, if you're not going to buy anything leave, this is a place of business I don't need the likes of you messing with my stuff; out!" he bellowed, pointing to the door.

Jamie's mouth fell open, angrily he said, "It's a wonder you make a living with that attitude, come on Nick I know when we're not wanted!"

He walked to the door, Nicky close behind, flung open the door and let it bang behind them.

"Can you believe him, how rude can people be, we weren't doing anything, and we might have bought something IF EVERYTHING WASN'T OVER PRICED?" Jamie said very loudly when he noticed the shopkeeper's face appear in the door window. He stuck his tongue out at him, put his arm around Nicky's shoulders and steered him down the street.

The boys passed the greengrocers and decided to pop in and say hello to Uncle Morton in the butchers shop. The shop was very bright and clean with white tiles on every wall from floor to ceiling; the floor was covered with sawdust. Hanging in the window were sides of beef and pork, while trays of sausages, meat pies, pork chops, stewing beef, mincemeat and whole chickens, all decorated with little pieces of parsley, lay in the display case.

There were four people milling around looking at the meat while waiting to be served when the boys entered. Uncle Morton was behind the counter serving a little old lady. Behind the counter with him was another man probably about 25 years old, who was serving the old man who had run out of the Post Office. Everyone stopped talking and looked at the boys.

Uncle Morton smiled at them and said, "What are you two doing here, where's your aunt?"

"We decided to come and look around the village and buy a postcard to send to the Stirlings!" Jamie answered.

"And Auntie said we could!" Nicky piped in.

"Well hang around a few minutes and I'll walk back up to the Mansion with you, it's nearly closing time."

Uncle Morton turned back and they could hear him saying "This is a really tender joint and it's just the right size for the two of you".

Uncle Morton and the other man finished serving the last customers and Uncle Morton walked over to the door and locked it, turning the "Open" sign to "Closed" as he did so.

He said, " Charlie, these are my nephews from London I've been telling you about, this is Jamie and this is Nicky, boys, this is Charlie Boyd I'm training him to be a butcher, so he can take over the shop when I retire."

"Hello boys, having fun?" Charlie smiled.

"Well we were, until we went into the hardware shop and that grouch told us to leave!" Jamie said, his anger rising again.

"And we weren't doing anything, I was even thinking about buying a penknife." Nicky added.

"I wonder what got into Herbert, he's not usually like that?" Uncle Morton said. He took off his navy and white striped apron and his white coat, hung them on the hook beside the big freezer, took down his coat and said, "Can I leave you to put the meat away and clean up, Charlie?"

"Sure you can Morton, you get off with the boys", answered Charlie cheerfully.

Jamie had the impression that Uncle Morton was trying to get them out of the village as quickly as possible. He wondered why.

Chapter Four

The Witchfinders

The boys decided to visit the graveyard right after breakfast the following morning to look for Charlotte's grave. Under clear blue skies, they walked out through the back door and along the service road, down the hill to the fork and past the school to the neatly kept graveyard. They entered through the arched gate in the four-foot high stonewall that surrounded the graveyard. A meandering path led to the little stone chapel and continued behind it.

The boys spent quite a while looking from gravestone to gravestone, but had no success. As they were about to walk around to the other side of the Chapel, an old lady came over to them.

"I've been watching you two, you look as if you're looking for someone in particular," she said softly, but with a distinct twinkle in her pale green eyes.

"Eh, yeah!" said Jamie "We're staying up at Whitehaven Manor and we were trying to find Charlotte's grave".

"Yes, I know who you are, but you won't find Charlotte's grave here, because she's not buried here." she said, in her soft voice.

"Where's she buried then?" asked Nicky.

"Not anywhere anyone will find her, thanks to her father." she answered, walking slowly away.

Even though she looked a hundred years old, was wearing an old fashioned grey dress and a black scarf draped over her head, the boys didn't want to lose the only person in the village who seemed to want to talk to them.

"So how much of the history of the Whitehavens do you know?" Jamie asked casually, catching up to her.

"The real story isn't about the Whitehavens, that's just a result of the real story, but you would never believe me if I did tell you the real story." she said, her green eyes flashing a challenge at them.

"Try us, we love good stories!" said Nicky, rising to the bait.

"You couldn't understand, you were raised with Normals, you'd have to be raised with our kind to understand." she replied, shaking her head and moving further away.

"What do you mean Normals?" asked Jamie frowning.

"Your mother didn't do you any favours by keeping you from the village, you're meant to be our salvation, but you know nothing." she said and shuffled away.

The boys looked at each other and Jamie made a circling motion at his temple with his finger. But Nicky wasn't so sure; he didn't think she was crazy; there was something in her eyes.

"Don't go, we really want to know what's going on, everyone's acting so weird, no-one talks to us and they all whisper behind their hands." Nicky said earnestly.

The old lady stopped and looked him straight in the eyes, he felt like she was searching his soul. Finally she smiled,

"Very well sweetie, I'll tell you the story, lets go and sit on the bench in the sun."

They walked slowly over to the bench and sat down beside her. She leant back against the bench, took a deep breath, and began her story.

"You've heard of the Witch Hunts in Medieval times?"

The boys nodded.

"Well, what a lot of people don't know is that they continued until the 17th century. But our story starts in the 14th century, when a wizard named John Padstow, tired of seeing innocent Normals as well as witches being executed on flimsy evidence, went looking for a place that could be hidden from the Witchfinders. He searched up and down England until he found a naturally fortified valley, surrounded on three sides by high rugged hills with the fourth open to the sea, with sheer cliffs to protect it. There was only one way in or out, a narrow gorge through the rugged hills; it was barely ten feet wide in places. Here, he decided was the perfect place to build a castle and, when word got out that he had found such a place, witches and wizards from all over England, wanted to join him. They were scared for their families you see, not knowing who they could trust. John even allowed Normals to join them because he knew that it wasn't only Specials who were dying. The person they had made medicine for last week, would turn them in this week for a handful of gold pieces. And so they came; they helped build the castle on the highest point over-looking the gorge. This became the symbol of their protection. They all felt safe within its walls." She paused and looked at the boys rapt faces and smiled.

"Over time the fear faded and people began to move out of the castle and build homes in the valley, they ploughed fields and grew crops and a village sprang up. Two hundred years passed and everyone lived without fear, they knew what was going on outside their valley but they were safe. Then a woman came to Simon Padstow and told him her cousin was being pursued by the witchfinder and wanted to know if he would be allowed into the village. Now there's one thing you two should realize about this village, this village was being protected by the Padstow Crystals.

No one could see the entrance or enter without someone from the village bringing him or her in. These crystals had brought prosperity and good health to the village, no one went hungry and no one died of horrible illnesses or accidents."

She stopped to see their reactions. Nicky was spellbound but Jamie was beginning to look a little sceptical. She smiled to herself and continued.

"They practiced white magic, mixed potions for broken bones, or spells when the cows couldn't give milk or chickens wouldn't lay eggs, but it was always for the good of the village. Now; the Padstow Crystals were always kept in the dungeon of the castle, only brought out if someone had left the village and got hurt, because these crystals on their own had magical healing powers, but together they were much more powerful. If they were to fall into a warlock's hands and used for black magic, no telling what could happen. But they were safe in the castle." "Anyway, lets get back to the cousin who wanted to come into the village. His name was Cyrus Ostrogoth. The village elders agreed to allow him in, so his cousin went out and brought him back. Everything was fine for a few years, but then people noticed that he had a fascination for black magic. He was called before the elders and asked to explain. He said that to understand the black arts, you had to study them, even practice them. The elders disagreed and they went to Simon Padstow for a decision. Simon's decision was final and he agreed with the elders, that the village had been built for the protection of the Specials and it was no place for black magic, if Cyrus Ostrogoth wanted to practice the black arts he would have to leave."

"Ostrogoth agreed to stop, but he was very angry. And soon the village would suffer for allowing him to stay. One September morning in 1596, Cyrus Ostrogoth left the village and met up with a witchfinder. He offered to betray the village for ten bags of gold sovereigns. Ostrogoth then led the witchfinder and thirty soldiers into the village. Because the villagers had felt so safe for 200 years, they scattered in panic when they saw the soldiers, instead of retreating to the safety of the castle. Some of the wizards, armed with sickles and scythes, stood and faced the soldiers to protect the women and children but were no match for the heavily armed soldiers. Once the last wizard fell, the soldiers turned on anyone left in the village. The witchfinder spent the rest of the day executing them all, men, women and children! Some were drowned in the traditional way and others were burnt at the stake. The soldiers set light to the village and the castle. Those villagers who had managed to escape to the hills watched in horror as their neighbours died and the village burned. The only house that they left standing was Cyrus Ostrogoth's with a message burnt into the door, one simple word 'BETRAYER'.

After the witchfinder's soldiers left, the villagers came down from the hills and retrieved the crystals from the ruined castle. Simon's wife, Gwendolyn, took one and went to heal and rejuvenate the villagers who had been drowned, while another villager took the other crystal to the entrance of the village to rejuvenate the wizards who had tried to protect the village, but he came across Ostrogoth sneaking back into the village. The villager confronted Ostrogoth and a fight broke out, the villager was killed, Ostrogoth grabbed the crystal, cursed the Padstows and fled. When Gwendolyn had finished at the pond, (because those burnt at the stake couldn't be revived), she went to help the villager at the entrance. After using the crystal to revive him, he told her what had happened. Among the wizards at the entrance, Gwendolyn found her husband, Simon. They worked through the night to revive all the wizards and by the morning there were one hundred dead, mostly the aged who had been burnt at the stake; luckily the children had been in school so they had escaped to the hills. Simon sent out word of the betrayal but no trace was found of Ostrogoth, some believed he went to Europe to practice the dark arts, some believed that he had died at the hands of some avenging wizard. As for the village, a very powerful spell was placed over it and only those who were born inside the village could see the entrance and bring someone in. As for the remaining crystal, Simon hid it, and its whereabouts was only told to the eldest heir."

"Wow, is that really true? Is there really magic and witches and stuff here?" Nicky asked wide-eyed.

Jamie looked even more sceptical and said, "Oh come on Nick, you don't really believe in that stuff, do you?"

The old lady winked and said "Don't knock what you don't understand young man!"

She rose from the bench and shuffled off around the side of the Chapel. The boys sat there for a few seconds, then Jamie yelled after her,

"Hang on, what was the curse he put on the Padstows?" He ran off around the chapel with Nicky in hot pursuit, but when they reached the other side, she was nowhere to be seen, there was only a grey tabby cat sauntering along the path. Jamie scratched his head and said,

"There's no-way she could move that fast, where's she gone?" Nicky shrugged his shoulders.

* * * *

In the kitchen, Auntie Lydia was preparing lunch and looked up as they entered.

"So, did you find Charlotte?" she asked.

"No, but we did meet an old lady," Jamie answered, his eyes sparkling, "she must have been a hundred at least and she told us a great story, didn't she, Nicky?"

"Mmm, I don't know anyone THAT old in the village, what did she look like?" she asked with a chuckle.

"Well..." Jamie thought, "She was very old, had whitish, greyish hair, she was wearing a long, grey dress [it was really old fashioned] and a black scarf over her head and shoulders, you know like one of those old fashioned things women used to wear years and years ago."

"That doesn't sound like anyone in the village" Lydia looked puzzled. "What was the story she told you?"

"It started back in medieval times when a wizard was tired of all the killings, so he found this valley and they built a castle then the village and about 200 years later this guy......" Jamie started excitedly,

"His name's Cyrus something" Nicky piped in,

"Yeah and he brought the Witchfinders into the village and they killed all the Specials... that's what she called them....."

"Not ALL of them, Jamie, or there wouldn't have been any one left to rejoov.... you know, bring them back from the dead." Nicky interrupted.

"Rejuvenate." Jamie said, "She said that there were two crystals called The Padstow Crystals and they used them to bring the people back to life. "

"Only the ones that weren't burnt at the stake!" Nicky interrupted again, "AND they only used one crystal because, remember, she said the bad guy stole the other one."

"Yeah that's right.... and the soldiers burnt down the village and the castle which Simon Padstow had built for the villagers' protection," continued Jamie.

"No, John Padstow built it, Simon Padstow tried to fight the soldiers and died, but he didn't really 'cos they used the crystal on him." Nicky corrected him again.

"Whatever! Anyway, after that this Cyrus guy got mad and put a curse on the Padstows, then the villagers put a spell over the valley to protect it from the Witchfinders." Jamie finished triumphantly.

Auntie Lydia got up from the table looking a little flustered and grabbed the kettle and placed it over the fire. Realising she hadn't added any water, she took if off again and hurried over to the sink to fill it, all the time avoiding the boys' eyes.

"Well… what a story!" she said with a nervous laugh, putting the kettle back on the fire.

"Yeah, she says there's still witches and wizards in the village!" Nicky said eagerly

"Well, I don't know about that, dear" she answered even more nervously and walked into the pantry.

Nicky and Jamie looked at each other and Jamie beckoned Nicky to follow him.

"We're just going to put our coats away, Auntie, we'll be back in a minute!" Jamie yelled over his shoulder as they ran out of kitchen and up to Jamie's room.

On reaching Jamie's room and closing the door behind them, they flopped down in the armchairs in front of the cold ashes in the fireplace.

Jamie said, "Did you see her reaction, she got all flustered, she knows something she's not saying!"

"OR.. she didn't want us to know the story. I bet it's true and there are witches here, that's why she acted all nervous like." Chirped in Nicky, his brown eyes glowing.

"You really think so? I don't believe it!" Jamie said doubtfully.

They both stared into the cold blackened hearth, deep in their own thoughts. What *had* made Auntie so nervous? Jamie thought.

Chapter Five

Auntie Amy Arrives

Monday morning came too quickly. The alarm went off beside Jamie's bed at half past seven; he rolled over and flung out his arm hitting the button on top. He rubbed his eyes. They had to go to school! He reluctantly threw back the covers, slipped out of bed, and stumbled, blurry-eyed, over to the open door and yelled,

"Nicky, it's time to get up, I'm going to have a wash first, okay?"

And, without waiting for a reply, he turned, walked to the other door and went out into the cold hallway.

The bathroom, which was next to Jamie's room, was quite old-fashioned, a claw foot bathtub stood to the left of the door; attached to the wall a few feet above the taps of the bathtub hung a small, round, "modern" electric water–heater, it's long, thin faucet protruding over the rim of the tub. The toilet, with an overhead tank and a chain hanging down, was just past the bathtub and opposite that was a small, oval-shaped sink set in an old, paint-chipped cabinet. On the wall beside the sink was a towel rack where different size towels hung. From the floor to half way up the wall, white tiles accented with a thin band of black tile went all around the room.

Jamie walked over to the sink and turned on the tap, there was only icy cold water, he looked longingly over at the water heater and made a mental note to ask his uncle how to turn it on. He quickly brushed his teeth and threw a few drops of water on his face. He grabbed the nearest towel, which was a little rough but smelled of fresh air, he lingered with his face in the towel for a few minutes soaking in the smell and remembering last summer when his mum had hung his T shirts on the line, they had smelled just like this. He hung the towel back up and dragged a comb through his unruly brown hair.

Jamie walked back to his room and asked Nicky if he was up yet, he got a grunt for an answer and said,

"The bathrooms free!" and quickly dressed. A few minutes later Nicky appeared at his door, washed and dressed, if still a little blurry eyed, and they went downstairs to the kitchen together. Auntie Lydia was just finishing pouring hot water into the teapot. On the table lay a platter of toast, a big box of cereal, a jug of milk, a pot of homemade jam, two glasses of orange juice and place settings for two.

She smiled as they entered and said,

"Sit, sit, tuck in! You don't want to be late for your first day of school, your uncle's already left."

"What time do we have to be there?" Nicky asked.

"Half past eight, you should give yourself fifteen minutes to get there", she replied smiling.

When the boys had finished eating, they shrugged into their coats, picked up their school bags and walked to the door. Auntie Lydia followed them saying,

"I'll see you at lunch time then, have a good day, bye boys!" She bent and kissed them on the forehead and watched them walk along the service road. Once they had passed through the gate and were no longer in sight, she shivered from the chilly morning air and returned to the warm kitchen.

At the road, the boys joined other children walking down the hill towards the school; these kids ignored the boys but greeted others coming up the hill from the village. A couple of the girls turned their heads to peek at the boys and then whispered to their giggling friends and when they reached the playground, most of children stood around and stared at them. Jamie and Nicky felt very uncomfortable with all their eyes on them, but they tried to act casually, even going so far as to say hello to some, only one pretty dark-haired girl smiled back and she got a dig in the ribs by her friend for doing so.

To make matters worse, when the bell finally rang and the children headed for the doors, Mrs. Pennith made a big deal when she saw them.

"Jamie, Nicky, there you are, come and stand beside me!" she said loudly as she opened the double doors to allow the children to pass inside.

Nicky turned pink, feeling all eyes upon him as he walked between the other children to stand at the top of the steps beside her.

"Come on children, don't dawdle, Jeremy pick up your coat and hang it up properly, Stephanie spit the gum out." Mrs. Pennith said sternly, as the boys waited beside her.

As the last straggler entered, she closed the doors behind them.

"These two pegs are empty so you can hang your coats here. It will be your responsibility to keep your belongings neat and tidy. Graham, what are you waiting for?"

"Sorry Ma'am, I left my homework at home, should I go and get it?" Graham answered shyly.

"No, you can bring it after lunch, but if you forget it again I will deduct 10 points from your overall score, now get to class." Relieved, Graham ran off and disappeared through the classroom door.

"There you go, Jamie," she said, leading Jamie to the classroom door. "Mr. Pennith is waiting for you; and Nicky, you come with me!" And she crossed the hallway to her classroom with Nicky in tow.

Mrs. Pennith pointed to an empty desk right in front of her, next to the pretty dark-haired girl who had smiled at them. Nicky quickly sat down feeling the blush coming on again. Mrs. Pennith greeted the children,

"Good morning children!"

"Good morning Ma am" was the response. Then she said,

"Today we have a new pupil, his name is Nicky Elder, and he comes from the mansion. Now I know we've never had a stranger here before, but I want you to treat him as if he was one of us." Nicky wished she would stop making him stand out but a few seconds later thought this was a very strange thing to say.

Jamie was going through almost the same thing himself. He was seated in front of Mr. Pennith, who started with the "Good morning" ritual, then proceeded to say,

"This is Jamie Elder from the mansion, he has come to stay with his Aunt and Uncle for awhile, and I would like you to treat him just like one of us." There were a few mumbles until Mr. Pennith clapped his hands together.

The morning went like any school morning; they had English until half past nine, then arithmetic until half past ten. Playtime (where the other children avoided them) until quarter to eleven, then back to class, where they studied Geography until twelve o' clock.

Jamie and Nicky met up at playtime and walked around the playground, trying not to look at the children who were still staring.

Nicky said, "Mrs. Pennith said something weird, she said she wanted the kids to treat me as if I was one of them, what d'ya think she meant?"

Jamie nodded his head excitedly, saying,

"That's almost the same thing Mr Pennith said". They both looked around at the other kids. "Well they look normal, apart from the staring!" Jamie said jokingly

"Yeah, I'm a bit concerned about the boy who sits a few rows over, I thought I saw an antenna coming out of his head, but it turned out to be a pencil he had behind his ear!" Nicky replied, grinning. Jamie grinned back; "And You know that Graham kid? Well, he dumped his whole bag onto the floor and you should have seen the stuff that came out of it! Mrs. Pennith hit the roof, it's a wonder you didn't hear her from your classroom."

The bell rang at that moment so there was no more time for talking, so they hurried over to the doors.

As the boys were leaving for lunch, Mr. and Mrs. Pennith called them over. Mr. Pennith said, "I don't think there's any need for you two to come back to school after lunch."

"Are we being expelled?" Jamie asked, his voice rising.

"No, no, Jamie," Mrs. Pennith said, chuckling. "The other children have projects to finish that they've been working on all year and you won't have anything to do, it's too late for you to start a project. So we'll see you tomorrow morning".

"Okay great!" Nicky replied, smiling

"It will give you a little more time to do your homework" Mr. Pennith said, with a wry smile.

The boys looked at him not sure if he was joking or not and then walked down the hallway to get their coats. By the time they reached the school gates, most of the children had gone. The ones that remained were eating sandwiches in the playground; a few others were playing tag.

At the fork in the road the boys saw Uncle Morton coming up the hill from the village, they waited for him to catch up and when he was in earshot, he said,

"How was school?"

"It wasn't bad, they told us not to go back this afternoon, something about the other kids finishing projects." Jamie said happily.

Uncle Morton replied smiling, "That's a bonus".

They all chuckled and continued up the hill. When they reached the kitchen door, they heard slightly raised voices coming from inside.

"I know Lydia, but what are we meant to do, she's safe for now, that's what matters!" said an unfamiliar female voice.

They heard Auntie Lydia reply, "But the boys…" her voice broke off as they opened the door.

Sitting at the table, her long, thin fingers wrapped around a mug of tea, was a skinny woman, dressed, in what could only be described as, hippy dress. She turned as the door opened and the boys caught the flash of emerald green eyes under long, reddish-brown eyelashes. A tie-dye scarf was tied around her forehead in an attempt to tame the thin, fly-away hair, which was the same colour as Auntie Lydia's. A long, baggy orange crocheted top hung to below her hips, and a belt, made of large coins tied together with thin leather straps, was tied loosely around her waist. Her skirt, which was also tie dyed in many colours, was full and flowing and nearly down to her ankles. She was wearing sandals, which struck the boys as strange, as it was still quite cold.

Uncle Morton walked forward with his arms out and said, "Amy you made it, how was the Retreat or was it a Spa this time?"

"Oh fine, just fine, nice and peaceful, just the way I like it!" she replied, walking into a hug. She looked over his shoulder and said,

"So these are Connie's boys, are they? Hi, I'm your Auntie Amy!"

She let go of Uncle Morton and held out her arms for the boys. They shyly walked into her embrace.

Auntie Lydia said, "I'm sorry boys, I got so wrapped up in talking with Amy, I forgot to make lunch, but we can have cold cuts, that won't take long and she bustled over to the pantry, just as Jamie replied

"Don't worry, we don't have to go back to school this afternoon".

"How come?" she asked, stopping in the doorway.

"The other kids have to finish some project or something." Nicky said.

"Well, that works out well, doesn't it, you can visit with me all afternoon?" said Auntie Amy, releasing the boys.

The boys took off their coats, threw them on the bench by the back door, and started setting the table. Jamie was watching Auntie Lydia closely; she seemed to be agitated and kept furtively looking over at her sister. Uncle Morton and Auntie Amy were chatting and laughing together. But Jamie's mind kept going back to the conversation they had interrupted. Who was safe? Were they talking about his mum? If so, why didn't Auntie Amy want to tell them? What was the big secret?

When Uncle Morton had gone back to work and the dishes had been cleaned away, Auntie Amy said, "I think I'll go upstairs and unpack and maybe have a nap, it was a long journey".

"I think we'll go outside and explore some more, if that's okay?" Jamie said.

"Yes, you go ahead, just be back for supper." Auntie Lydia answered mechanically.

The boys picked up their coats and walked through the back door. They went through the gate in the wall and headed for the summerhouse. When they were sure they were out of earshot, Jamie said,

"Do you think they were talking about mum?"

Nicky nodded but didn't say anything. He was watching the grey tabby-cat sitting on a fence post, hunting.

Then Jamie said, thoughtfully "Well, at least she's safe".

Nicky still didn't say anything.

The boys reached the woods, then the summerhouse, in silence. They popped out the screws and scrambled through the window. Nicky walked over and sat down on the wicker couch.

Jamie looked over at him and said, "What's the matter, you're very quiet?"

Nicky shrugged his shoulders but didn't say anything. Jamie came over and sat down beside him, much softer this time, Jamie asked, "What's wrong?"

Nicky's bottom lip quivered, but he just shook his head. Jamie waited, watching him trying to control his emotions.

Eventually, Nicky said quietly, "It's been so long since I saw mum. I was beginning to forget about her... you know.. with everything that's going on.... and now I feel really bad 'cos she might've been dead or some'ut... and dad ...we still don't know if he's alive...and we don't know for sure they were talking about mum… they could have been talking about anyone and I miss them so bad…… I just want to go home!" He turned his head away so Jamie couldn't see the tears running down his cheeks.

Jamie began to feel really bad too. Getting wrapped up in the witches story and the strange villagers had pushed his parents predicament out of his mind, but now all that didn't seem important. He decided he was going to talk to his uncle, he wanted to see if Uncle Morton would have the same reaction as Auntie Lydia or whether he would give him some straight answers.

They stayed in the summerhouse for about an hour, trying to clean it up, but without a broom it seemed to be useless. Jamie suggested they find the path leading down to the beach and go and play down there for a while. Nicky agreed and they set off. It wasn't hard, the path was just a few feet away from the broken window and they followed the steps down. The steps were carved out of the cliff itself and were quite steep. The handrail was wobbly and parts were missing, but the boys stayed against the cliff and were down at the bottom in no time. The beach was actually a small pebbly cove with high cliffs to the left and right, which jutted out into the sea. The only way onto it was from the sea or down the steep steps. Jamie and Nicky stayed on the beach, skipping pebbles and trying to build sandcastles, for about two hours, then headed back for supper.

The boys entered the kitchen, their hair a total mess and their cheeks bright red from the cold wind. As usual, Auntie Lydia was cooking. She looked up as they entered, but didn't say anything, which Jamie found quite strange; she looked angry, she had little pink spots on her cheeks and her hands were trembling. At that moment, Auntie Amy came out of the pantry carrying carrots, cauliflower and broccoli. She too looked angry, but she tried to put on a smile for the boys. "You must have been on the beach, to get those rosy cheeks!" she commented.

"Yeah we were! Can we set the table or some'ut" Jamie asked, feeling he had to say something.

"Yes please, we'll eat in the dining room today as there's five of us".

She saw the puzzled look on Jamie's face and said, "Through the Butler's Pantry," and she pointed to a door beside the stove. Nicky and Jamie collected the cutlery and dishes and walked through the door into the Butlers Pantry.

The Butlers Pantry was a small narrow room with a fireplace on one wall and a door in the far corner; this they assumed led to the dining room. Covering the whole length of the opposite wall was a bank of cupboards and shelving. There was nothing else in the room. The boys walked to the door and into the dining room. This room was the same layout as the morning room except it had a highly polished wood table in the centre with matching chairs; the seats were of straw stuffed tapestry that was beginning to fray. The top half of the walls were covered in red satin wallpaper and the lower half was dark wood panelling. The floorboards were a rich oak and looked as if they had been well looked after. Jamie wondered how come this room seemed to hold its former glory when the rest of the mansion hadn't.

The boys finished setting the table and returned to the kitchen. By now the vegetables were steaming and Auntie Lydia had a basket of fresh buns and the butter dish ready for them to take through.

Auntie Lydia said, "After you've taken these through, you two might as well go upstairs and get washed up for supper, we'll be eating as soon as your uncle gets home."

So the boys went upstairs to Jamie's room, a fire had recently been lit in the grate, but the room still felt chilly. Jamie picked up his hairbrush and tried to get his hair to lay down but the wind had done a good job on it, so he decided to go and wash it. While he did this, Nicky walked into his room where a fire had also been lit and changed into a dry pair of jeans and socks, as he had got a little too close to a wave and got soaked up to his knees. His jeans had almost dried but his socks were still wet.

When he had changed, he walked back into Jamie's room just as Jamie came back, shivering, with his hair soaked and a towel around his neck.

Jamie said, "I definitely need to ask Uncle Morton how that emersion heater works, I'm tired of washing in cold water and I'm definitely not having a freezing cold bath".

He dried his hair and ran the brush through it again and put on a clean T-shirt while Nicky went to wash. Afterwards, they walked back downstairs together. Uncle Morton had already arrived by the time they reached the kitchen and he greeted them warmly. They helped carry the last few dishes of food to the dining room and then they all sat down to eat.

"How was everyone's day?" Uncle Morton asked trying to break the silence.

"Great, we went down to the beach for a while." Nicky answered.

"How was your's dear?" Uncle Morton asked Auntie Lydia.

"Fine!" she answered curtly.

Uncle Morton scrutinized her face and decided not to press her, so he turned his attention to Amy.

"And what have you been doing?"

"Just getting settled in, nothing much!" she gave a furtive look at Lydia but Lydia didn't look up from her plate.

The boys looked at each other feeling very uncomfortable. The dinner was soon over and their aunts went off to the kitchen. This gave Jamie the opportunity to ask his uncle some questions.

"Uncle" Jamie began "Can you show us how the emersion heater works tonight, I had to wash my hair in freezing cold water?"

"Oh sorry Jamie, I meant to show you days ago, you should have reminded me".

"Uncle!" He tried again "Um … err… do you… err I mean, have you heard anything about our parents?" he finally blurted out.

Uncle Morton looked at him in surprise and said,

"Oh I thought you had been told, I don't know why they haven't told you…. Maybe I shouldn't say anything?" he said, looking very uncomfortable, but when he saw the look in their eyes, he relaxed and smiled,

"Yes, there was a sighting of your mum, she seems to be alright but no actual word from her herself yet, but I'm sure it's just a matter of time. She loves you two very much and she wouldn't stay away from you unless she had to, you know that, don't you?"

"But what made her go, why did she leave us and where's dad?" Nicky asked, feeling the knot in his throat again.

"I can't answer that, I wish I could, I do know he's not with Connie, but I can't tell you anymore than that." He looked at Nicky's sad face, so to try and cheer him up he said,

"Shall we play a game this evening, we've got quite a few board games and some playing cards?"

"Yeah, maybe," Nicky said gloomily.

"I'll show you how that heater works first though, shall I?" said Uncle Morton with forced cheerfulness as he rose from the table. Jamie did likewise and followed him upstairs, but Nicky stayed seated and was left alone in the dining room.

After sitting gloomily for a few minutes, he got up and followed Jamie and Uncle Morton through the Conservatory and Portrait Gallery, then into the Front Hall and up the staircase. He reached the bathroom door just as Jamie and Uncle Morton came out.

Nicky said "I think I'll take a bath if that's okay?" then, as an after thought, "The water IS hot, right?"

Uncle Morton nodded and showed Nicky how to work the emersion heater, he then began running hot water from the heater and cold from the tap into the bathtub.

"Don't fill the bath too full or you will run out of hot water. Also this jug here," and he reach inside the cabinet under the sink and came up with an old cracked water pitcher, "in the mornings, if you fill it with hot water, you can fill the sink so you don't have to wash with cold water."

When the bath was nearly half full, Uncle Morton turned off the taps and tested the water. He said, "Okay, there's the towels, facecloth and soap, is there anything else you need, no? Okay then enjoy your bath" and walked out of the bathroom, followed by Jamie.

Nicky went to his room to get clean pyjamas, his dressing gown and slippers. He had learnt that you had to wear your dressing gown and slippers if you didn't want to freeze to death.

Nicky returned to the bathroom and locked the door; he got undressed and climbed into the soothing warm water. He had been soaking for about twenty minutes when he thought he heard someone try the door handle. He looked at the doorknob and sure enough it was turning

He yelled, "Is that you Jamie?" no answer, he yelled again, "Who's there?..... you're not funny Jamie!"...... still no answer.

He watched the knob slowly turn back and then stop, he listened to hear footsteps but heard nothing. He jumped out of the bathtub, grabbed a big towel, wrapped it around his waist, and unlocked the door. There was no one in the hallway, he opened Jamie's door but there was no one there either. He went back into the bathroom, relocked the door and climbed back into the bathtub, very puzzled.

He remained in the bathtub until the water turned cold and then got out, while he was drying himself off, there was a knock on the door and Jamie's voice asked. "Have you drowned yourself in there or something?"

"No, just drying off, but wait for me!". He quickly dressed and unlocked the door, "Did you come upstairs and try the door handle a little while ago?"

"No why" Jamie asked curiously.

"Well someone did, I saw the handle move, but no one answered when I called out."

"Well it wasn't me" Jamie said, shrugging.

The boys were now at the top of the grand staircase, they went down them two at a time, crossed the Front Hall and entered the Morning Room, which the family used as a living room because the Salon was way too big. Uncle Morton was sitting at a card table with a board game in front of him, an empty chair sat opposite him. Auntie Lydia was sitting in an armchair beside the fireplace, knitting, and Auntie Amy was sitting on the couch in front of the fireplace, crocheting.

"Come and warm yourself by the fire" Auntie Amy said, patting the couch beside her.

He walked to the couch and sat down, feeling the warmth of the fire. Jamie rejoined Uncle Morton at the card table and they began a lively game of Snakes 'N Ladders.

"Did anyone come upstairs and try the door knob while I was in the bathtub?" Nicky asked, looking from face to face. They all replied no. He thought that this was strange, if no one here did, and there's no one else in the house, how could the doorknob turn?

Chapter Six

The Rose

The rest of the week was almost identical to Monday, each lunchtime Jamie and Nicky were told not to come back to school until the following morning. They spent the afternoons either exploring the estate or in the summerhouse. The boys had managed to sneak a broom and dustpan out of the house. If the weather was bad they would go to Nicky's room and read Charlotte's diaries, they had sneaked them into the house without anyone seeing and the boys had told Auntie Lydia that they would clean their own rooms so that she wouldn't find them. The only problem with that was, it meant they actually *had* to clean their rooms, at least once a week.

On Thursday afternoon, which was a particularly awful day, the rain poured down as if someone had turned on a shower and the wind blew so hard that it almost blew them off their feet as they tried to get home from school.

After a most delicious lunch, Jamie and Nicky decided to look for a hiding place in their rooms. They started with the fireplace in Jamie's room as it had the same design of acorns under the mantelpiece as the one in the child's room. They pushed every single one but nothing popped open, so they went and tried the fireplace in Nicky's room. This wasn't as ornate as the others, it had only dental mouldings and two lions heads carved from wood, one on either end holding up the mantelshelf.

Nicky was comparing the lions' heads while Jamie began pressing all the "teeth" on the dental molding. Nicky compared the noses, they looked the same but he pressed them anyway, he compared the manes, looking for a switch, a lever or something, they were identical, but no switch or lever!

"I'm beginning to think this is a waste of time," Jamie said, half way along the molding.

"Just keep pressing, I can't believe they would only put one secret hiding place in one fireplace in the whole mansion, can you?" Nicky said, scrutinising the teeth. "Hang on!"

"What?" Jamie said excitedly.

"Look at this" said Nicky, pointing to the canine tooth on one of the lions' heads.

"It's higher!" Jamie said, a grin appearing on his face.

Nick pressed it but it didn't move, he pulled it towards him, still nothing, then he pushed it away and there was a slight scraping noise.

"Did'ya hear that?"

"Yeah, it came from here!" Jamie said, looking at the side of the fireplace. "Look!"

Nicky saw what Jamie saw, the side of the fireplace was slightly open! Jamie opened the door wider to reveal three shelves hidden behind it.

"Great, we've found it!" Nicky beamed.

"Now all we have to do is sneak back into the North Wing and retrieve Agatha's Spell Book." Jamie said happily.

They placed Charlotte's diaries on the top shelf and pushed the door closed. They left Nicky's room, crept silently down the stairs and peeped around the corner to see if the hallway was clear. Auntie and Uncle's room was the closest to the third floor stairs, quickly the boys tiptoed past it, then past Auntie Amy's room.

The coast was still clear, so they slipped down the stairs, up the other side, and behind the tapestry. It was pitch black, but they knew where they were going this time. The boys headed for the third floor staircase. At the top they made their way to the child's room, pushed open the creaky door and entered. The room looked the same as it did before. Closing the door behind them, Jamie walked over to the fireplace and pressed the raised acorn, the drawer scraped open.

"What the......!" Jamie exclaimed.

"What?" Nicky asked.

"It's gone, it's bleedin' well gone"

"What? The book?" Nicky said peering in the draw.

What a shock Agatha's Spell Book had gone, they looked at each bewildered.

"Who the hell took it" Jamie yelled, "No-one knew it was there, only us".

"Shush someone might hear you!" Nicky whispered and looked towards the door as if expecting it to fly open at any moment.

But Jamie wasn't listening. "How could it disappear"? He said, stomping around the room.

"I don't know but if you don't stop stomping I'm sure we'll find out pretty soon."

Jamie stopped and looked at him. "Sorry! But I'm mad!"

"No kidding; really?" Nicky said sarcastically. Jamie was just about to yell again, when he saw the twinkle in Nicky's eyes and smiled instead.

Now that he had managed to get Jamie calmed down, Nicky looked around the room and said,

"Wasn't that doll on the dresser over there last time?" pointing to a doll on the table by the cold fireplace.

Jamie, who was still immersed in the disappearance of the book, said, "Who cares?"

"No Jamie look! That doll has been moved, you can see where it used to sit, there's no dust there!"

He had walked over to the dresser and was looking down among the other dolls. Jamie walked over, curious now, and said,

"You know what this means? Someone else has been in here, moved the doll and took the damn book!"

"No duh!" Nicky replied, "I *had* worked that out myself!"

"Maybe Auntie Amy, she's been here long enough to go snooping?" Jamie said.

"But she lives here why would she start snooping now? She couldn't possibly've known we had found the book, it looked like it hadn't been moved for years!.

"Auntie Lydia knew we had been on this side, we told her" said Jamie.

"Yeah, I guess it could've been her, but she made us promise not to come back here, didn't she?"

"Yeah, we really kept that promise didn't we?" Jamie smiled… and Nicky smiled back.

"We'd better get going before some one does comes!" He said.

Just as they reached the door and pulled it open, Jamie saw something flutter in the corner of the room behind the door, he bent down and picked it up. It was a page from Agatha's Spell Book. At the top it read "Rejuvenating Spell – To Bring Dead Plants Back to Life". Jamie skimmed through it quickly and followed Nicky out the door.

"What's that?" Nicky asked.

"It's a page from Agatha's Spell Book, it must have fallen out when they took it".

"Let me have a look." Nicky said.

"Wait until we get back to your room." Jamie said, stuffing it into his pocket.

They retraced their steps back to Nicky's room, Uncle Morton had lit the fire at lunchtime when he learned the boys were planning on staying in their rooms to do homework for the afternoon, and now the room was toasty warm. The boys sat in the armchairs in front of the roaring fire, homework forgotten. Jamie read out;

> *"Rejuvenating Spell – To Bring Dead Plants Back to Life*
> *_____(name of plant) wilted and dead,*
> *With loving hands I tend your bed.*
> *Come back to life and show me your heart,*
> *For you are too beautiful for us to part."*

"Let's try it on these dried flowers" Nicky said rushing over to the vase of dried flowers by the window.

"Oh come on Nicky, you really don't think it's going to work do you?"

"There's only one way to find out." Nicky said grinning. He reached over and lifted out a dead rose. He walked back to Jamie and placed the rose on the table between them. Jamie scoffed,

"This is stupid, it's not going to work!"

"Then I'll do it, gimme the spell", said Nicky stubbornly. He snatched the piece of paper out of Jamie's hand, raised it slightly over the rose and read out the spell. Nothing happened.

"See, told ya!" Jamie said triumphantly.

"Hang on a minute….. maybe you have to be holding the rose", said Nicky and he picked up the rose and repeated the spell. He thought one petal turned a little redder. He said "Did ya see that?" pointing to the petal.

"That's probably just the reflection of the fire OR your imagination!" Jamie said, still unconvinced.

So Nicky got up and walked to the window. Standing facing the window with the rose held up he read the spell again. All of a sudden he felt a strange vibration going through his fingers and the rose began to shimmer and the stem started to feel soft between his fingers, he could see the thorns growing up the stem, then the leaves became green and supple and the rosebud turned from almost black into a soft rich red.

He stood there stunned, not believing what he had just seen; slowly he turned to Jamie who was still sitting by the fireplace shaking his head at him. As he turned the rose came into view and Jamie stopped shaking his head, jumped up and, in three bounds, was beside Nicky

"What did you do with the dead one?" he said looking around "You must've switched 'um."

"It's magic! it works! *There is* such a thing as magic, see!" Nicky said excitedly holding out the rose for Jamie to see.

Jamie gingerly took it and felt the moistness of the petals, the sharpness of the thorns and the suppleness of the stem. He stammered "But how?… Magic isn't real!"

He was mesmerised by the beauty of the rose, he realised that he had never before looked at how delicate the petals of a flower were. Nicky had actually brought it back to life! He just couldn't take his eyes off of it.

While Jamie sat transfixed, Nicky found a vase in Jamie's room and filled it with water. He took the rose from Jamie and placed it lovingly in the vase, then placed it on the table between the two armchairs and sat down. They both stared unbelievingly at the beautiful, live, vibrant flower.

* * * *

Long after Nicky had gone to bed and fallen into a deep sleep, he dreamt he was walking down the grand staircase and there at the bottom stood his mum with her arms outstretched and in one hand, she was holding the most beautiful red rose. He ran down the stairs, fell into her embrace, and heard her say,

"Well done Nicky, you have inherited your mother's gift!" But it wasn't his mother's voice at all, it was the old lady's, from the graveyard. He gave a yell and suddenly found himself bolt upright in bed. He searched the darkness but could see nothing, he thought he heard a slight click and then a cold draught washed over him. He heard Jamie stumbling towards the door.

"What's the matter, why did you yell?" Jamie asked.

"The old lady, she was here, I know she was, she spoke to me!" Nicky said, breathing very fast.

"What old lady, there's no one here?" Jamie said.

"The old lady from the graveyard, she was here, I know she was, she spoke to me" Nicky insisted.

"You must've been dreaming!" Jamie said, finally finding a match to light the oil lamp beside Nicky's bed.

"Yes I was, about mum, but the voice was real, it spoke right into my ear, that's what woke me up and then I heard a click and felt a cold draught as if someone had opened and closed the door. I'm not imagining things, Jamie, honest!" Nicky pleaded.

"Okay! okay! what did the voice say?" Jamie asked.

"It said something like, 'Well done, you've inherited your mum's gift.' " said Nicky.

"What's that supposed to mean?" Jamie asked.

"I think it had something to do with the rose, 'cos in my dream, mum was holding a red rose!"

"Well there you go, I told you, you were dreaming, and see there's no one here now. How about I lock your door just in case. Now, you go back to sleep, we have school in a couple of hours."

He walked over to the door turned the key and walked back to Nicky "Do you want me to leave the lamp lit?" He asked kindly. Nicky nodded and laid back down, pulling the covers up around his ears. Jamie put the lamp back down beside the bed, said goodnight and went back to his room.

Nicky lay there for ages with thoughts whirling around inside his head. Had he been dreaming? No, the voice was real, she was here, but how did she get in? Who was she? How did she know what he had done? It must have been a dream, but it was so real, and the click, he HAD heard the click *and* felt the cold draught, there was no mistaking that. Around and around they went until he finally fell into a fretful sleep.

Chapter Seven

The Search for Charlotte

Nicky woke the next morning with a pounding headache and blurry eyes. He staggered out of bed and over to Jamie's room. Jamie was just slipping his feet into his slippers as Nicky entered. He took one look at him and, in two strides, was beside him. He put his hand on his forehead like he had seen his mum do many times.

"You're burning hot!"

"I've got a really bad headache and I can't keep my eyes open." Nicky replied weakly.

"Go back to bed, I'll go and get Auntie!" Jamie steered Nicky back to his room.

He found Auntie Lydia in the kitchen pouring tea for Uncle Morton. They looked up in surprise as Jamie entered, dressed only in his pyjamas.

"I think Nicky's sick, can you come and look at him?" Jamie asked.

Auntie Lydia quickly put down the teapot and hurried after Jamie. In a few minutes they were beside Nicky's bed.

With a sympathetic smile she said, "So what's the matter dear?"

"My head hurts and I'm really tired" Nicky replied quietly.

She put the back of her hand on Nicky's forehead and said, "You're a little warm, you might have caught a chill yesterday. Just to be safe you better stay in bed today. I'll bring you up something for the headache and some soup in a little while, try and go back to sleep".

Nicky nodded and closed his eyes. Auntie Lydia pulled the covers up around his chin and smoothed them out. She beckoned Jamie to follow her into his room.

"I don't think it's anything serious, but I think he should stay in bed at least for this morning, tell Mrs. Pennith he's sick and don't you worry, he'll be fine".

"But shouldn't I stay home and look after him?" Jamie asked, feeling it was his responsibility as his parents weren't there.

"No dear, you go to school, I'll take good care of him," she said smiling "Anyway you'll be home at lunchtime and then you can sit with him, he'll probably sleep most of the morning after I have given him a po… portion of medicine." she corrected herself quickly.

Jamie washed, dressed, and just before going downstairs, looked in on Nicky who was fast asleep. He tiptoed out of the room and ran down to the kitchen for breakfast.

"He's asleep," he said upon seeing his Auntie.

"Good, that's what he needs, here's your breakfast dear, you had better hurry or you're going to be late for school", she said, looking up at the clock.

He bolted down his breakfast, grabbed a piece of toast, stuck it in his mouth while he took his coat down from the hook beside the door and ran out, trying to get his arms into his coat. There was a loud hiss as he tripped over the grey tabby sitting right outside the door.

"Stupid cat!" Jamie muttered as he hurried up the path.

Auntie Lydia picked up the coalscuttle and ash pan and quietly crept back into Nicky's room. He was fast asleep; she walked over to the fire bent down, and proceeded to clean out the grate. Then she lit a fire, made sure it was burning nicely and slipped out of the room without waking Nicky. At ten o'clock, she was placing the last thing, a piping hot bowl of chicken soup, onto a tray. She picked up the tray and carried it upstairs, quietly opened Nicky's door and crossed the room to his bedside table where she laid the tray down. She looked down at Nicky, felt his forehead again and he opened his eyes.

She smiled kindly and said, "You have a little fever dear, put this under your tongue!"

He opened his mouth and she slid a thermometer under his tongue. After a couple of minutes she took the thermometer out and read it, shook it and put it back in its case. She picked up a green bottle from the tray, removed the cork and poured some thick red liquid onto a large spoon.

"Open up, this will make you feel better in no time".

Nicky opened his mouth, screwed up his nose and swallowed the liquid. But to his surprise it tasted quite good, sort of like strawberries but different. She then placed the cork back in the bottle and said,

"Are you ready for something to eat?"

Nicky looked over at the tray and nodded. She helped him sit up, propped up his pillows behind him, and handed him the bowl of chicken soup. He ate about half and handed the bowl back.

"I think I'll go back to sleep now. Thanks" he said, turning on his side and laying back down.

"That's a good idea, the medicine will make you sleepy and before you know it, Jamie will be home."

She stood up; the fire was making the room stuffy; so she opened the window just a little, to let in some fresh air, then picked up the tray and tiptoed out of the room.

Nicky's eyes were already feeling heavy, so he closed them and drifted off to sleep. The birds' songs coming through the open window danced around in his head and faded away, a seagull suddenly squawked as it flew by, the fire crackled in the fireplace, a whiff of fresh air came through the window. He heard them all but couldn't bring himself fully awake.

After a moment or two, he became aware of a weight on the bottom of the bed and tried to push it off. He forced open one blurry eye; the grey tabby cat was sitting there looking at him.

"Wha'you doing here?" he mumbled, but his eyes became too heavy and he closed them again and drifted back to sleep.

The cat stretched, jumped silently from the bed, sauntered over to the blazing fire and curled up in front of it.

Nicky fell into a deep sleep. He awoke two hours later, stretched, opened his eyes and stared at the drapes of his bed. He became aware that he was not alone and looked over at the fire, which was now no more than embers. He sat up slowly and blinked.

"How'd you get in here?" he said, looking around at the closed doors "Wha'do you want?"

Sitting in one of the overstuffed armchairs in front of the fire was the old lady from the graveyard, still in her old-fashioned, grey dress.

"I heard you were sick and wanted to see if you were alright. This is a very pretty rose." She replied, looking down at the rose beside her. "I see your aunt gave you some strawberry flavoured Chill-out Potion".

"Huh?" Nicky said.

"Medicine in the green bottle, tasted like strawberries, she gave you some, didn't she?"

"Err… yeah, it tasted good!" Nicky answered.

The old lady rose from the chair and walked towards the door, saying,

"As long as she's looking after you then!" and she slipped out into the hallway.

He stared after her. Not more than thirty seconds later, Jamie came into the room carrying the coalscuttle.

"Did you see her?" Nicky asked.

"See who?" Jamie asked as he threw some coal onto the dying fire.

"The old lady, she was just here, you must have passed her in the hallway, she's only just left!"

"There was no one in the hallway," Jamie said, coming over and putting his hand on his forehead.

"I'm not delirious, she was really here, I don't know how you could've missed her. Unless... unless she went into one of the other bedrooms when she heard you coming?"

Jamie looked at him in disbelief and Nicky said angrily,

"Why don't you ever believe me, first you didn't believe me when I told you someone had turned the bathroom doorknob, then you didn't believe me when I told you she was in my room last night and you don't believe me now! "

"Okay, okay, if you say she was here, I believe you!" Jamie said, unconvincingly.

"No you don't!.... you think I'm making it all up; well I'm not and I don't care what you think, I hate you, GET OUT OF MY ROOM!!" Nicky yelled hysterically.

"*Calm down*, before you give yourself a heart attack! I'm not saying I don't believe you, it just seems strange that this old lady can get in and out of the house without anyone but you seeing her!" Jamie said soothingly.

"Well maybe she doesn't want anyone else to see her, you acted like you didn't believe her in the graveyard and that's probably why she doesn't want to SEE YOU!" Nicky said sulkily.

"Well next time she shows up, ask her what her name is and what the Padstow curse was will ya." Jamie said lightly, trying to get Nicky to smile.

But he wouldn't smile, he was too angry. Jamie decided the best thing was to leave him to sulk, so picking up the poker; he poked the fire to loosen the ashes. When the fire sprung to life, he picked up the coalscuttle and threw some more coal on it.

"I'm going down for some lunch, do you want me to come up and play a game with you after?"

"Whatever!" was the only answer he got, so he left.

Nicky lay in his bed feeling really angry with Jamie. He threw back the covers and slipped his feet into his slippers, pulled the heavy quilt from his bed, wrapped it around himself and sat in the overstuffed armchair by the now roaring fire. He absentmindedly picked up the rose and was feeling the petals when a thought came into his head. Why not practice and turn some more flowers back to life. He threw the quilt off and crossed the room to the window where the vase of dried flowers stood. He looked at them and picked up a yellow daisy, held it up to the window and said;

> *"Yellow daisy wilted and dead,*
> *With loving hands I tend your bed.*
> *Come back to life and show me your heart,*
> *For you are too beautiful for us to part."*

Again he felt the vibration through his fingers and the daisy began to shimmer, the stem felt soft and supple, pale green leaves began to sprout from it and the petals turned a bright vibrant yellow. He touched the petals, they were soft and moist. He felt much happier now. He could do magic! Nicky dropped the daisy into the vase with the rose, picked up another daisy and repeated the spell; again it came to life. He went through all the flowers in the vase that he knew the names of and when he had finished the vase was full of colourful, vibrant flowers.

He felt exuberant and wished he had Agatha's Spell Book to see if he could do other spells. A soft knock on the door made him jump; he quickly pulled the quilt around himself and said, "Come in!"

Auntie Amy came in bearing a tray loaded with food. "I thought you might be hungry, so I brought up a little of everything!"

As she walked towards him he lifted the vase off the table and placed it beside the fire so his aunt could lay down the tray.

"What beautiful flowers, they smell so sweet, where did you get them?" she asked casually.

"Err.. errr… I don't know, they were here when we arrived" Nicky said, guiltily.

"Well, they have lasted a long time, they look like they've just been picked." she said, smiling and looking at the flowers.

Nicky picked up a cup of tea and began to drink it hoping that she wouldn't be able to see his guilty face. To his dismay, she sat down in the armchair beside him, picked up the poker and knocked ash through the grate, making the flames jump to life. The room was feeling very warm and cosy; Nicky pushed the quilt off his shoulders. Auntie Amy reached over, put her hand on his forehead, and smiled.

"The medicine seems to have worked, how are you feeling?" she asked.

"Much better thank you. That medicine Auntie gave me…. was it Strawberry Flavoured Chill Out Potion?' he asked matter-of-factly.

"What?…" she stammered "A potion, what a silly idea, of course it wasn't, where would we get a po'… I mean what put that into your head? You must have had some very strange dreams dear."

"I guess I did, I thought I read it on the label, but my head was hurting so bad, I probably did dream it."

It was her turn to blush guiltily. She rose from the chair, mumbled something about having to go back down stairs and rushed out of the room. Nicky sat there for quite some time thinking and wishing that Jamie had been there to see her reaction. He knew Jamie wouldn't believe him if he told him, so he decided he wasn't going to tell him. Nicky decided he was going to find the old lady on his own, because she knew a lot of ways to get in and out of the house without being seen and he wanted to know how she knew so much of what was going on inside.

Nicky had been picking at the food on the tray while these thoughts occupied his mind and before he knew it he had eaten almost everything on the tray, the only thing that was left was a lovely Eccles cake, which he was just about to pick up when Jamie poked his head around the door.

"Still mad at me?" he asked, making faces.

"A little!" Nicky replied, trying not to laugh.

"Can I come in, is it safe?" Jamie said, pretending to be scared as he walked into the room. "Wow! look at the flowers, where'd you get them?"

"From over there." Nicky replied nonchalantly, pointing to the nearly empty vase of dried flowers by the window.

"You changed all these?" Jamie was dumbfounded.

"Yep, all with MAGIC that doesn't exit!" Nicky said, puffing out his chest.

"Okay, you've convinced me, magic exists! I believed after the rose, Nick." Jamie said smiling.

The boys were soon back to their old selves, laughing and joking together, planning what to do next. They came to the decision that the pages they found in the summerhouse must have come from another diary Charlotte had written after the two they had found, so they were going to search for it or any further ones. Nicky suggested that a good place to hide a book would be with other books and they agreed they should search the library.

The next morning was Saturday, Uncle Morton went off as usual to the butcher's shop and the boys' aunts decided to go to the nearest town, which was about ten miles away, to do some shopping; Auntie Lydia wanted some more wool and Auntie Amy needed a new pair of shoes. The boys declined the offer to accompany them, saying Nicky wasn't really up to it yet, when really, of course, they wanted the time to explore the library. A worried look crossed Auntie Lydia's face and she said that maybe she shouldn't go if he still wasn't feeling well, but Jamie assured her that he was quite capable of looking after him, so his aunts shouldn't worry, he would be fine. So feeling reassured, they left for a day of shopping.

The boys hurried into the library as soon as they heard the old station wagon drive away down the gravel driveway. They watched from the window as it turned onto the road and disappeared from sight, and then turned their attention to the wall of books.

Now and then one of them would bring down a book, read a few pages and put in back, moving on to the next promising-looking book. Jamie found a book called "The History of the Padstows", written by a Prudence Neville; it was hand written in 1728. They decided this was a keeper and put it on the table.

Nicky next found a book named, "Potions Through the Ages", which he opened and, after reading a couple of pages, decided that this was a keeper too. Jamie came across a book that didn't have a name on it but when he opened it, he found another book inside; it was Charlotte's diary, dated 1901 – 1902. They searched for a bit longer without finding anything of real interest, Jamie glanced down at his watch and, realising that Uncle Morton would be home soon for lunch, they snatched up the books and ran off to Nicky's room to hide them.

They hurried back downstairs and had just finished making a pot of tea when the kitchen door opened and Uncle Morton strolled in. Nicky appeared out of the pantry with a tray of food Auntie Lydia had left for lunch.

Seeing Nicky up and about Uncle Morton asked "Feeling better?"

Nicky smiled, nodded, and placed the tray of food on the table. Jamie poured tea and they all sat down to enjoy the lunch. As soon as Uncle Morton had left for work again, the boys ran back up to Nicky's room and, before settling down to read their new finds, Jamie poked the cinders, threw a couple of sticks of kindling on them and, when they caught, put a couple of pieces of coal on.

Jamie started with "A History of the Padstows" and Nicky with "Potions Through the Ages".

Nicky was reading all the ingredients needed to make a potion to cure warts. He said, "Yuk!" and turned the page.

"Hey, this is what Auntie gave me!" he said, excitedly.

"What is?" Jamie asked, distractedly.

"This…Strawberry Flavoured Chill Out Potion, that's what the old lady said she gave me…. it sure worked!" Nicky said happily.

Jamie looked up again. "What are you talking about?"

"This, moron! This is the potion that auntie gave me!" he said getting a little peeved.

"Auntie didn't give you a potion".

"Yes she did!" Nicky said hotly, "it was thick and red and tasted like strawberries and the old lady said it was this Strawberry Flavoured Chill Out Potion… Oh what's the point! You don't believe anything I tell you!"

"I believe you! I believe you! Calm down!" Jamie said soothingly. He leant over and read over Nicky's arm. "Sounds disgusting to me!" and went back to reading his book again.

They sat reading for quite some time, until Jamie broke the silence by saying, "That story the old lady told us, it's right here, I've just finished reading it."

He was beginning to think that maybe everything he had been taught in history class was only half the story. He had never believed in witches and thought it was all superstitious nonsense. But now he wasn't so sure! Nicky had made dead flowers come to life, he had seen him do it with his own eyes [though still found it hard to believe!] And Auntie had given Nicky a potion that had made him better in a matter of hours instead of days. And now this book confirmed the story that the old lady had told them.

Jamie turned back to the book and said, "Here's the curse that Cyrus Ostrogoth put on the Padstows, it says, *"May no Padstow heir be born under the veil of protection"*. I wonder what the "veil of protection" is?

"I guess that explains why the Padstow name stopped hundreds of years ago, because no boys were born." Nicky said.

Nicky had looked up from his book when Jamie began talking; something on the table against the wall behind Jamie caught his eye. "What's that?" he asked.

"What?" Jamie replied, turning around to look were Nicky was pointing. Nicky got up and walked over to the table, picked up a small velvet, drawstring bag and a piece of paper.

He said. "Listen to this;

"I've gathered and prepared the ingredients for you so all you have to do is the spell.

The Repair Spell (For objects made of wood)

Gather the ingredients,
Grind to fine dust.
Recite the spell.
Sprinkle dust simultaneously

Bark of the tree,
Earth from Beneath,
With dust from an elf,
Repair thyself

.

Try it Nicky"

Who's it from?" Jamie asked, rising and walking over to Nicky and reading over his shoulder.

"Dunno, there's no name!" Nicky said, but deep down he was sure it was the old lady. "I'm going to try it, I need something made of wood that's broken." He looked around his room but couldn't see anything.

"There's a wobbly table in my room, want to use that?" Jamie said.

Excitedly, they ran into Jamie's room and over to the wobbly table leaning against the wall. Jamie removed the photo of his mum and the doily and pulled the table away from the wall. Then he held the paper for Nicky, who stuck his hand in the bag and pulled out a handful of fine sparkly dust. Nicky held the table with his left hand, looked at the paper Jamie was holding and began to recite the spell, at the same time sprinkling the table with the dust.

The dust fell very slowly; each particle shimmered as it caught the light, when it touched the table it seemed to evaporate into the wood. As Nicky finished reciting, he stopped sprinkling and let go of the table. Jamie placed the palm of his hand on the table and tried to wobble it but it was solid.

"Wow! it worked, let me see if I can do it?" Jamie said excitedly.

"Okay but we need something else that's broken" said Nicky.

"Let's check out the other rooms, there must be more broken stuff around here, everything needs repairing." Jamie said.

The boys crossed the hall to the first room, everything was under dustcovers, they couldn't find anything that needed repairing so they moved to the next room, this was also under dustcovers but, as the first, nothing needed repairing, the only other room on this floor was the turret room, so they decided to try their luck there.

They walked to the end of the hallway and opened the heavy door. This room was full to the brim with old tables and chairs, couches and sideboards, beds and dressers, wardrobes and side tables; some looked to be in good shape, others looked banged up and some were broken. Jamie chose a chair with a broken leg, which he pulled to a small clearing in the room and, while Nicky held the paper, Jamie held the leg to the chair, took a handful of the dust and recited the spell. At first it didn't look like anything was happening, the dust shimmered and then evaporated just like before but the leg didn't re-attach itself. Jamie's face dropped and he was just about to say it hadn't worked when he felt the leg begin to get warm and it got warmer and warmer, he began to think that if it got much hotter he'd have to let it go, when suddenly, with a jerk, the leg re-attached to the chair, with no sign that it had ever been broken.

He looked at Nicky with a huge grin on his face and said, "I can do it too, did'ya see? I did it too!"

Nicky grinned back at him and said, "I guess you've got mum's gift too, huh?"

Jamie wanted to do another and then another, he was so excited and he hadn't had as much fun in ages. He never realised how exhilarating it had been for Nicky and why Nicky wanted to try something else, but now he did, he didn't want to stop, but Nicky brought him back to earth quite sharply when he said,

"We had better stop, or someone's going to notice all this stuff isn't broken anymore".

So Jamie had one more look at his handy work, then followed Nicky back to his room. Sitting back in the armchairs by the fireplace, Nicky picked up "Potions Through the Ages" again and started flipping through the pages, while Jamie added a few more coals to the fire, before picking up Charlotte's diary.

Nicky stopped at a potion and smiled and said, "I know how the dining room table and stuff looks so nice!".

Jamie looked up and Nicky read;

"Restore Old Furniture to New Potion

> *1 lb   Beeswax*
> *8 oz   Sap (from the type of tree*
> *furniture is made from)*
> *4 tbsp Hemlock*
> *1 tbsp Liverwort*
> *2 hairs from a Unicorn tail*
> *4 tsp   Lemon juice (for fragrance)*
> *Place beeswax in pot to melt.*
> *Grind sap to fine dust. Add sap*

dust, hemlock and Liverwort.
Simmer for two hours. Add
Unicorn hairs. Continue to
simmer for approx. three days.
Remove from heat, add lemon
juice and cool slightly. Pour into
wide neck jars to cool and harden
completely.

Rub small amount over entire
surface, buff to a shine. Scratches
and dents will disappear."

"Maybe they should use it on some of the other furniture around here, it could really use it!" Jamie said, looking around the room. He went back to reading Charlotte's diary. The first entry was October 1901, Jamie said, "Listen to this;

Dear Diary,

Daddy found me in the summerhouse writing to
you and ripped up my diary and then he boarded up the
summerhouse so I cannot go there anymore. I wish mummy
were still alive, she wouldn't let daddy do this. He has
become so mean since she died. Now Aunt Agatha has
disappeared. I found out that he had her locked up in this
room he has me locked up in now. He said she was mad
and no one can be brought back once they are dead. He
hasn't learnt anything living in this village, he is so narrow-
minded.

Mrs Crabb is being mean too, just because I won't marry her horrible brother, she keeps forgetting to bring me my meals and if she does, there's not much of it."

Jamie then flipped over a couple of pages and began reading aloud again.

"30th November, 1901

Dear Diary;

Daddy still refuses to let me out, he doesn't even come and see me anymore, he just sends Mrs Crabb, she wants to get hold of the estate so bad, I wouldn't be surprised if, after I'm forced to marry her horrible brother, she didn't poison daddy and me. But I will never marry him. Daddy doesn't seem to see what she's like, he just sees the money her horrible brother is dangling in front of his face."

He skipped through a few more pages and continued reading;

"15th December, 1901

Dear Diary;

Daddy says if I agree to marry Mr Horrible he'll let me out and we'll have a nice Christmas together. But I will not marry him.

I've been reading Aunt Agatha's book, she wrote down a spell that she was working on to unlock the door so she could escape but she says she hasn't perfected it yet. If daddy doesn't let me out soon, I am going to try it, though Aunt Agatha says it's very dangerous, that's why she wanted it perfect, but I don't care anymore if I die trying, at least it will be all over."

Jamie skipped to May

"Dear Diary;

I'm so unhappy I don't think daddy is ever going to let me out, I look out the window and smell the fresh air and long to run through the woods to the summerhouse or run along the beach and feel the wind in my hair.

Mrs. Crabb only brings me one meal a day now, she refuses to bring me clean water to wash every morning, so I have to use as little as possible because I don't know when she's going to bring me some more. I told Mrs. Crabb that Aunt Emily would come back from Europe soon and rescue me."

"23rd May

Dear Diary;

Daddy came to see me today, he said that Aunt Emily and Uncle Robert have been killed in Europe and there is no one to rescue me and my only way out is to marry Mr. Horrible. I have no other choice now but to try Aunt Agatha's spell, it must have worked because she got away,

*didn't she? I'm going to try it tonight when everyone is
asleep, by the time they find I'm missing I could be half way
to London."*

"That's the last entry, so either she tried it and got away or
she tried it and that's how the damage happened and she died."
said Jamie with finality to his voice. He closed the book and put
it on his lap.

Nicky looked at him and said hopefully, "She might have
still got away, even if she blew up the room, one side of the room
was fine".

"I doubt it Nick, don't you usually stand right up against the
thing when you're doing a spell?" Jamie said.

Nicky nodded his head sadly.

"So you think she died, then her dad must have buried her
somewhere on the estate, because the villagers would have started
asking questions, he was a Normal and I bet they didn't trust
him. Hey! Hang on a minute, he lied! He said her Aunt and
Uncle died in Europe but they couldn't have 'cos we're here, her
Aunt Emily was the sister whose family tree continued remember,
Agatha never had kids"

The boys sat and pondered what they had learned. Agatha
had disappeared or died, Charlotte did or didn't blow up the
room, did or didn't die and was or wasn't mysteriously buried.
Nothing seemed any clearer than before they read the diary, but

it did look like this was the end. There wouldn't be any more diaries to find.

Little did they realise they had only scratched the surface of this mystery, soon they would find someone to explain everything to them and it would be more exciting than anything they could imagine. And would lead them to understand why their parents, also, had disappeared.

Chapter Eight

The Secret Passage

Daylight crept through the gap in the thick velvet curtains and lay across Jamie's face. He slowly opened one eye and turned away from the light but it was too late, sleep had already left him and he knew he wouldn't be able to get it back. He stretched and lay there listening to Nicky's soft snoring coming from the other room. He had promised Uncle that he would help him fix the lawnmower today.

Jamie slowly sat up and stretched again. The room was chilly and he reached for his dressing gown lying at the bottom of his bed. As he pulled it towards him something fluttered to the floor, he reached down and picked up a piece of paper. Scrawled on it in delicate handwriting, were just a couple of words, "Well done Jamie". He looked at it and re-read it. He didn't know what to make of it. What had he done well? Who was it from?

From Nicky's room he heard a loud yawn; he slipped his feet into his slippers, put on his dressing gown and walked over to Nicky's room. Nicky was sitting up in bed rubbing his eyes; he looked over as Jamie entered.

"Mornin' " Nicky said.

"Mornin' " Jamie replied and sat on Nicky's bed, "Look at this!" Jamie handed him the piece of paper.

"Oh, that's from the old lady!" Nicky said, casually.

"How do you know it's from her, her name's not on it?" Jamie said logically.

"I dunno, I just do, who else would leave it?"

Jamie shrugged his shoulders and stuffed it into his dressing gown pocket.

Fifteen minutes later, washed and dressed, the boys followed the smell of bacon all the way to the kitchen where their aunties and uncle were just putting breakfast on the table.

"Perfect timing, breakfast is ready!" Auntie Lydia said, smiling at the boys.

"Do you want tea or orange juice, boys?" Auntie Amy asked.

"Orange juice, please." Nicky answered, holding up his glass.

"Me too, please" Jamie said, tucking into a big plate of egg, bacon, fried bread and fried tomatoes.

After breakfast Jamie and Uncle Morton left through the kitchen door and crossed the courtyard to the stables. Uncle Morton pulled open the old dilapidated doors, inside Jamie saw a large tractor-style lawnmower, not the little electric one he was expecting. When he thought about it he realised that there probably wasn't anywhere to plug one in. He walked over to the lawnmower with Uncle Morton and watched while Uncle Morton lifted the bonnet and started tinkering with the engine. He asked Jamie to pass him some tools and soon they were discussing what could be wrong with it. Jamie had always been fascinated by engines and had thought he'd like to be a mechanic when he grew up.

Back in the kitchen Nicky was helping Auntie Amy with the dishes while Auntie Lydia put them away. When he had finished, he slipped away to the library and quietly closed the door behind him. He didn't want to be disturbed; he had decided to look for more clues to Charlotte's disappearance, because he didn't believe she had died in the explosion.

Nicky began going through the books on the right side of the fireplace. He was pulling each one out, looking inside just in case there was another book tucked inside. He reached for the book closest to the fireplace but it seemed to be stuck. He pulled again but it wouldn't budge. Bending forward to take a closer look, Nicky realised that it wasn't a book at all but a block of wood disguised as a book, right down to the leather covering. He thought this very strange and when he tried to pull it off the shelf again, he heard a slight click and the bookshelf sprang open just a fraction. He stepped back and pulled, it was very heavy with all the books but he managed to pull it wide enough to peer behind.

Hidden by the bookcase was a door-sized opening made of very large square stones with an arched top. He stepped inside and immediately to the right was a flight of steps leading down into pitch darkness. He needed a light, so he backed out and looked around the room. There was an oil lamp sitting on the mantelpiece that he hadn't noticed before right beside a box of matches, "How convenient is that?" he thought.

With the oil lamp lit, Nicky slipped in behind the bookcase again and pulled it up behind him; he didn't want anyone discovering him there. He slowly made his way down the very worn, very cold, stone steps, every footfall echoing deep below him and, with the lamp held above his head and his other hand against the rough stone wall, he followed the steps round and round, descending lower and lower under the mansion.

At the bottom he found himself in a wide passage. There was a strange smell coming from somewhere further along, he wasn't sure what it was, it smelt like something very old, like the smell you get in abandoned buildings, but also maybe a bit like stew and maybe some burning wood thrown into the mix too. He wasn't sure; all the smells seemed to mingle together.

He crept along the passage, not sure why he felt the need to be very quiet, the air became warmer and the aroma of stew cooking was replacing the old smell. The passage turned and let out into a large chamber, Nicky stopped to take in the sight. The chamber's ceiling was about fifteen feet high and was held up by rows of square pillars spaced about ten feet apart and the top of each pillar splayed out to form arches from one pillar to the next on all four sides, creating the effect of rows of arches. As he walked around, a feeling of peace and contentment came over him and he thought how nice it would be to stay here forever.

"AAAAHH!!" He yelled and jumped sideways as something rubbed up against his leg. He looked down, his heart pounding in his chest, but it was just the grey tabby cat.

"You again!" he said

"You do seem to keep finding my secrets, don't you?" said a voice.

He swung around but there was no one there. Except the cat, he shook his head, what was he thinking, cats don't talk.

"Who said that?" he said, loudly this time.

"I did!" came the reply.

And this time he *knew* it had come from the cat, he had seen it's mouth move. But he knew that was impossible. As he stared dumbfounded at the cat, it seemed to be growing larger, and larger still, it's legs became longer and its paws began to look like hands and then the fur on its head turned into white hair. Before he knew it, the old lady from the graveyard stood before him.

Nicky staggered back in complete shock, his mouth open and his eyes bulging from their sockets. The old lady smiled and said,

"It's okay you're not imaging things you really did see me change from a cat".

He just stared at her as she shuffled over to him and put her hand under his arm and gently steered him to a chair. Nicky fell into it and sat there staring at her with his mouth still open.

"Close your mouth dear!" she said smiling and he clamped his mouth shut. "Snap out of it sweetie, you know magic exists, you've done it yourself and very well I might add."

He still sat there staring at her; she sat down in an old armchair a couple of feet away from him and waited for him to speak. Shortly he found his tongue and mumbled, "How?"

"Ahh! The first question is always "how?" I've been around for a long time and had plenty of time to practice.," she answered.

"Who?" was the next thing he managed to mumble.

"And that's always the second question. Let me introduce myself, my name is Charlotte Whitehaven." she said, formally.

Again the dumbfounded look appeared on Nicky's face. But this time he shook his head to clear it and said,

"I knew you hadn't died in that room, but we had given up hope of finding out what happened to you, when your diary ended." He blushed realising that he had been reading someone's diary that was still alive.

"That's alright, I wanted someone to read them and care what happened to me, that's why I put them in the library and summerhouse all those years ago. But you two were the only ones who found them." She said as if she had read his mind

"Yes but…. you must be…" he counted in his head, "…over a hundred years old if you were sixteen in 1901!"

"That's right sweetie, I'm old but I don't feel it, I think it must be the crystal". She said.

"The crystal is here" Nicky said looking around.

"Somewhere I believe, I haven't found it yet, Simon hid it after Ostrogoth stole the other one. The hiding place was handed down from mother to daughter, but when my grandmother realised that Agatha wasn't quite right, she passed it onto my mother, then she died in a riding accident and my father wouldn't let Agatha bring her back, so I never learnt of its hiding place." she said.

"So what happened that night you decided to use Agatha's spell to get out?" Nicky asked.

"I think I should tell both you and your brother together as you both have worked very hard to find me." she said smiling at his crestfallen face.

Nicky grudgingly nodded and asked, "Where have you been living all these years?"

"Right here, I'd found the cellars a long time before my father locked me away, but I knew that he didn't know that the Manor had been built on the ruins of the old castle because he wasn't interested in our history, so I hid down here, I collected broken furniture and fixed them and made my home down here, come and see."

Charlotte led Nicky into another chamber slightly smaller but still with the pillars and archways. This chamber felt very cosy, a large faded rug covered the floor in the centre and atop that stood a large, square, chunky kitchen table; tucked up close were four ill matching chairs that were very dainty compared to the table. At the far end of the chamber, the giant fireplace from the original kitchen of the castle stood proud, pots were hanging from hooks over the blazing fire and that aroma of stew was emanating from one of them.

To one side of the fireplace a big old armchair with a high back sat and beside that a bulky wooden table; on the opposite side of the fireplace, a large cabinet and sideboard stood slightly in the shadows. Between three of the archways, Charlotte had hung tapestries to form a bedroom, there was a four-poster bed surrounded by red velvet curtains and a large wardrobe. The whole area was bathed in warm candlelight and the shadows from the pillars fell large across the floor.

Nicky took in every detail and was in awe of the wonderful comfortable feeling he had, it was like visiting the perfect grandmother's home, the cosy warmth and the aroma of something delicious cooking. Nicky never wanted to leave.

Just then something caught his eye beside the sideboard; it was a very old, worn black pot, a smile crossed his face, was that really a cauldron?

The small kettle hanging on a hook over the fire began to sing; Charlotte shuffled over to the wooden cabinet and on a tray placed two chipped cups, a sugar bowl, a milk jug, a teapot, a tea caddy, and two mince pies on a plate. She carefully lifted the kettle from the fire and poured water into the teapot. Charlotte noticed the frown on Nicky's face and said, sheepishly "I'm sure your aunt would have given them to me if she knew I was here, dear".

Nicky drank his tea, conscious of Charlotte watching him.

 "Did you leave the spells and the notes?"

"Yes dear, when I saw how well you did with the rose, I knew you had inherited your mothers gift, so I wanted to encourage you", she answered.

"You keep saying that but my mum doesn't have a gift, she's just a normal mum" Nicky said puzzled.

"No dear, your mother is a Special and she is the most talented out of the three of them, I had great hopes for her as a girl, I nearly told her my secret, but then I overheard an argument between her and her mother, she wanted to be Normal she said, and to go to college in London. Her mum didn't want her to go, but in the end she went and never came back, such a waste!" Charlotte said sadly.

Nicky took in this piece of information for a few minutes then asked, "How did you see me with the rose, we were alone in my room?"

"I was in the field trying to catch my supper, I looked up, and you were standing at the window, I have excellent eye sight as a cat", she answered.

"Catch your supper?" Nicky said, horrified.

"Yes dear, how else do you expect me to eat? I do cook it after I've killed it. I hunt and move around the house as a cat because I'm more agile then, I usually only change back down here."

"So what's in the pot?" Nicky gulped thinking the worst.

"Rabbit stew!" she said smiling.

"If you've finished your tea, you should be off or they will start looking for you. Don't forget to bring your brother tonight after everyone's gone to bed, I'll be waiting for you."

"Just one more thing" Nicky said placing his cup on the table "My aunts; can they do magic too?"

"Yes dear, all descendants of the Padstows can, some are more powerful than others. Lydia is sweet natured but she doesn't have your mother's gift, she can do the odd spell, but her talent is making excellent potions. As for Amy, well she spends too much time abroad with foreign witches, I haven't seen her do anything for a long time, except of course, the travelling spell."

"What about Uncle Morton?" Nicky asked.

"Your uncle…. well he's a Normal, but he knows all about your aunts, he grew up in the village, his family was one of the original Normal families allowed in with John Padstow. John allowed about fifty Normal families in, over time Normals and Specials married and their children and children's' children would have the gift while others would not, your uncle's family for instance, his mother had the gift but he doesn't! Now, you must go quickly!" she said, shooing him to the stairs.

Nicky quickly ran up the steps, at the top he stopped, put out the lamp, placed it on the floor and listened for any sound in the library. It was quiet, so he opened the bookcase and slipped back out. He left the library and opened the front door, quietly closing it behind him and went in search of Jamie.

He found him in the courtyard, having a driving lesson on the tractor and enjoying every minute of it. Nicky watched for a while and then decided he would tell him later and went off into the field. Nicky walked up onto the veranda and sat down on the low wall, remembering that this was the first place he had seen the cat. The veranda, which spanned the length of the Mansion, had grass growing between the stone slabs, every six feet or so, urn style flowerpots sat on the wall; some were cracked, some had weeds growing out of them and others were just empty. Nicky wished he knew a spell to make the veranda look nice again.

Auntie Amy came out through the conservatory with a tray of glasses and a pitcher of lemonade that she placed on a rickety old wicker table close to Nicky; he thought it was going to break under the weight and wondered why no one had used the repair spell on it. Uncle Morton and Jamie came through the gate at that moment, Jamie was grinning from ear to ear.

"That was awesome," he was saying and seeing Nicky, he said, "Uncle let me ride all around the courtyard on the lawnmower until I got the hang of it, he says I can cut the grass in a couple of weeks when its dried out".

As he sat down on the wall next to Nicky and took a glass of lemonade that Auntie Amy handed him, Uncle Morton came out of the conservatory carrying a couple of wicker chairs which he placed around the rickety table. Nicky reached over and took a glass and so did Uncle Morton. The veranda was protected from the wind by the high ivy-covered wall and the sun shone quite warmly down on them, they could see the grass swaying on the lawn further away. Auntie Lydia came and joined them and they all sat there, enjoying the sunshine after the storms of the last couple of days.

Nicky saw the grey cat sauntering through the long grass and wondered what she was up to now. He had smelled her dinner cooking so he didn't think she could be hunting. She disappeared into the woods. Uncle Morton was explaining to their aunts what a great help Jamie was and Nicky caught Jamie's eye and said, between closed lips, "Must talk to you!".

Jamie nodded. Uncle Morton turned to Nicky and said, "And what have you been doing with yourself while Jamie's been helping me?"

"Nothing really" Nicky lied.

They finished their lemonade, Jamie said, "Let's go for a wander", and boys got up and strolled away. When they were out of earshot, Jamie said, "So wha'cha want to tell me?"

"You won't believe me, but I found Charlotte and I'm going to take you to see her after everyone's gone to bed!" Nicky said proudly.

"Why after everyone's gone to bed?" Jamie asked.

"Because I don't want anyone to miss us", Nicky replied.

"It's Sunday so everyone will be going to bed early." Jamie said. They strolled back towards the mansion and entered through the open doors of the conservatory.

* * * *

Jamie and Nicky said good night about quarter past nine and went up to their rooms, they had a wash and got into their pyjamas then waited for the house to go quiet. At ten thirty Nicky felt it was safe to leave, so he called softly to Jamie, who appeared almost immediately at the door. The boys slipped down the stairs, only using one oil lamp to light their way. When they reached the second floor they extinguished the lamp, peered around the corner and looked down at the bottom of the bedroom doors; there was no light showing under them, so they tiptoed past and along the hallway, down the staircase and across the Front Hall to the library.

Nicky closed the door soundlessly behind Jamie and beckoned him to the fireplace. He relit the oil lamp and touched the book;

a slight click was heard, the bookcase sprang open and Nicky pulled it open far enough for him to pass through. Jamie stood there for a few seconds in surprise then quickly followed Nicky, who had already started down the stone steps. When they reached the small chamber, Charlotte wasn't there but the tabby cat was. Nicky smiled because he new what she was going to do.

"Well?" Jamie asked.

"Well what?" came the soft purring voice of the cat.

Jamie stared at the cat and looked at Nicky, Nicky began to smile, the cat began to change just like she had before and Jamie stood there completely dumbfounded. Nicky led Jamie to a chair and pushed him down into it.

He said, "I would like to introduce you to Charlotte Whitehaven".

Jamie just stared, Charlotte smiled and Nicky began to laugh.

"It's very rude to stare!" Charlotte said to Jamie, still smiling.

"But… how… your….but…. I don't……" Jamie stammered, Nicky wiped the tears from his eyes.

"Close your mouth Jamie, a bus is coming," he laughed. Jamie transferred his stare from Charlotte to Nicky

"How did you…?." Jamie stammered again, indicating to Charlotte.

"By accident!" Nicky answered.

"Accident?"

"Yeah I was looking for clues in the library....."

"Boys we don't have a lot of time, if you be quiet I'll tell you my story." she said softly, sitting down in the comfy chair by the fire. Nicky pulled a chair up close to her. "So this is my story! I am assuming you've read my last diary?" The boys turned a slight shade of pink, "As I told Nicky, that's okay, I wanted someone to read them. So are you ready?" The boys nodded. "Okay then. After I had learnt the spell, or thought I had would be a better way of putting it, I decided I was going to try that night. I waited until midnight when I knew everyone would be in bed, I went to the door and recited the spell and as soon as I did I knew something was wrong. The room began to vibrate horribly so I hid beside the big wardrobe hoping it would protect me. What I didn't realise was that the spell was also changing me, I began to feel I was shrinking and my face grew fur on it, my instincts became sharper and so was my fear. I was thinking like a cat, my instincts told me I was in danger so I squeezed behind the wardrobe for protection and then suddenly there was a huge bang, half the wall collapsed and the roof fell in on me, if it wasn't for the wardrobe I would have been crushed. I was so scared, my heart was pounding so loud in my ears that I panicked, the door had been blown completely off its hinges so I ran, I ran as fast as I could, I tripped up Mrs. Crabb as I ran along the hallway, she was coming to see what the noise was, I ran all the way down to the conservatory! I was beginning to feel trapped and then I noticed one of the windows was still open so I jumped through it and took off across the lawns to the one place I always felt safe, the summerhouse. But I couldn't get in because I didn't know how to change back, so I climbed the big oak tree as high as I could and found a nook to curl up in. I felt safe there because I was so high I could see all the way to the manor, in fact I could see everything because I had cats eyes! I saw mice scurrying through the grass, nests of birds, I could smell food miles away. I saw my father look over the broken wall to see if I was lying on the ground, I heard Mrs. Crabb calling to me. I stayed a cat for many months, I didn't know how to change back and I was scared that they would find me. At night I would creep back into the mansion and steal food from the kitchen, Mrs. Crabb had a habit of not cleaning up after dinner, so there were lots of scraps and once she left a whole roast beef sitting on the table. I had a very full tummy that night!" Charlotte smiled. "Then one day, sitting in my usual place in the tree, I realised I could change back and it was because I wasn't scared anymore. I also started begging at the kitchen door to see if Mrs. Crabb would recognise me, but she only saw a cat. She was kind to me as a cat too, she would give me scraps and milk and once, when it was raining, she let me come into the kitchen and curl up by the stove to get warm. But the weather was turning cold and I knew I had to find somewhere else to stay; the summerhouse would be cold, so I decided I would hide in the cellar, this cellar. Neither Mrs Crabb nor my father knew about it so I knew I would be safe. So one day when she left the kitchen door open while I ate the scraps she had put out for me and went off to do something, I snuck into the house and hid in the north wing. I waited for everyone to go to bed, what I didn't know was my father had taken to drinking too much and most nights would fall asleep in the dining room, so while my father was getting drunk in the dining room and Mrs. Crabb went up to bed, I snuck back down to the library, changed, let myself in and then opened the secret door to the cellars. Over the years, I have collected bits and pieces of furniture, that the family didn't want, usually because it was broken, so I fixed them all and made myself a home here."

"Your dad never looked for you?" asked Jamie shocked.

"Well he did to start off with, but I think he thought I had blown myself up. The villagers were getting a little hostile too; they thought he had killed me along with Aunt Agatha. The only person who stuck by him was Mrs. Crabb but even she left a couple of months before my dad died, he drank himself to death you know, she made a quick exit one night never to be seen again. No one went to my fathers funeral, they were glad the outsiders were gone."

"How do you know that?" asked Nicky.

"I used to go into the village, as a cat, and listen to the villagers conversations. They really disliked my father and Mrs. Crabb, they wanted to run them out of the village long before my father died, but calmer heads prevailed and they were allowed to stay, but no one would talk to them, I started to feel sorry for Mrs. Crabb, I really don't know why she stuck around as long as she did, but after she left, my father spent all his time in the tower room (the one he locked me in) and just drank. Then one night, he was drunk as usual, he was standing at the broken wall looking out across the lawn and he staggered and fell. The farmer's son found him the next morning when he brought his sheep over to graze on the lawns. He went and got his father."

"How do you know he was drinking and stumbled?" asked Jamie.

"I was in my tree, I had taken to watching him from there, because even though he was mean to me, he was my father and I still loved him. I saw him fall, I ran over and he wasn't dead when I got there. I changed and he looked at me... then he said, " Charlotte I'm sorry...!" and... he died!."

She went quiet for a moment and the boys didn't say anything.

"There was nothing I could do and I wasn't ready for anyone to know I was alive, so I sat with him, I knew they would find him in the morning, when I heard the farmer's son coming, I changed to the cat and watched, they took him away and the next day they buried him."

"Wow that must've been really hard to see your dad fall like that." Jamie said softly.

"Yes it was! I grieved for a long time, remember I was only seventeen and now I was all on my own."

"But what about your aunt and uncle, your dad lied about them dyeing in Europe." Nicky said.

"Yes, you're right, I found that out later. Word got to them that my dad had died and they came home to run the estate. They didn't know anything about my disappearance until after they got back, they thought they would find me here and would look after me, but by that time I was a little wild and couldn't go back to the strict Victorian upbringing that I saw my cousins living, so I stayed down here."

"What happened to Agatha? Did your dad kill her?" Nicky asked.

"I don't know dear, I've never found out what happened. All I know is that she was locked up in the tower and then one day she was gone." She leaned against the back of the chair and closed her eyes. The firelight showed the age lines on her face and she looked very tired. The boys sat and looked at her, waiting for her to speak, not wanting to say anything unless she had fallen asleep. Her eyes opened and shone bright green like a cats.

"Well that's my story, I think you two have a story of your own, don't you?" she asked.

The boys shrugged their shoulders.

"They still haven't told you?" she said disgustedly, "I think its time you showed them what you can do and demand to be told what's going on, you have the right to know and the ability to help. Now it's time for you to go back to bed and don't tell anyone I'm here, I still like my freedom, but you could bring me some of the wonderful food I keep smelling, especially the bread!" she said, smiling.

The boys crept back upstairs to their bedrooms, it was now almost midnight and they had to get up for school in seven and a half hours. They reached their rooms, said goodnight to each other, climbed exhaustedly under the covers, and were soon fast asleep.

Chapter Nine

The Truth Be Told

The morning came all too soon for the boys. It seemed to Jamie as if he had just closed his eyes when the alarm clock went off. He dragged himself out of bed and staggered to the bathroom. They ate their breakfast in silence and soon found themselves walking to school. At least it was only half the day, Jamie was sure he wouldn't be able to make the whole day and looking at Nicky he was dead sure he wouldn't. They didn't discuss the meeting with Charlotte; there was much too much to discuss on the short walk to school, they would have all afternoon to do that.

Geography dragged on, Nicky only heard half of what Mrs. Pennith was saying and history wasn't much better. Thank goodness for playtime, at least they could get some fresh air and maybe wake up a bit. Arithmetic went a little better, but thankfully lunchtime arrived.

During the walk home the boys discussed a strategy to bring up the subject of magic, which they were going to put into practice right after lunch. They met Uncle Morton coming up the hill and they all walked home together, they ate lunch, afterwards Uncle Morton returned to the butchers shop, leaving the boys with their aunts. Nicky left the kitchen and returned a few minutes later, Jamie gave a slightly nervous cough and said,

"Aunties, we have something to discuss with you."

Their aunts looked at each other bewildered and sat back down at the table. Nicky walked back through the doorway carrying the vase of dried flowers, the vase of living flowers, the rickety old table from the veranda and the two spells that Charlotte had given them. He placed these on the table opposite his aunts and stood next to Jamie.

Jamie began "We have found out a lot about our heritage and this village and before you start interrupting" he said quickly, as he saw Auntie Lydia about to object, "we want to tell you that we are okay with it, in fact we think its great and we want to show you something."

He nodded to Nicky. Nicky picked out a dried Iris (Jamie had found out what it was from a flower book) he held it up and recited the Rejuvenating Spell, then placed it in front of his aunts, who sat there looking at it. Both started to speak at the same time but Jamie, raising his voice slightly to be heard, interrupted,

"Wait, we haven't finished yet!"

Jamie took a handful of dust out of the velvet bag, touched the rickety table and recited the spell; the table became as sturdy as a rock. Again the aunts tried to say something and again Jamie shushed them.

He said, "Now you've seen that we can do magic, please don't try telling us that it doesn't exist. We know you and mum are witches and so are most of the people in the village. We found out about the Padstow curse, how the north turret was damaged, what happened to the crystals and that one is still meant to be hidden here by Simon Padstow. What we don't know and what we really want to know is, what's happened to mum and dad and why?"

The aunts looked at each other again, and Auntie Lydia said, "It's what I've been saying all along, its high time they were told the truth, they've been kept in the dark way too long, and see what's happened, they found out anyway. We're lucky they weren't taken too."

With a sigh, Auntie Amy replied, "Alright dears, I will tell you everything that I know!"

"It started before you were born. What you may not know is that your mum got tired of hiding away in this village, she wanted to know what it was like on the outside. So she left and went to London. We tried to stop her, we told her it would be dangerous, but she was always head strong. Ostrogoth, she said, had disappeared and no one had heard anything of him for years"

"Ostrogoth, you mean the guy who brought the witchfinder into the valley?" asked Jamie.

"Yes dear, one and the same!" answered Auntie Amy.

"But there's no way he could still be alive, that happened hundreds of years ago!"

"Let us finish, it will all be clear shortly" Auntie Lydia said calmly.

Auntie Amy continued,

"Where was I, oh yes, she met and married your dad and tried to live as a Normal, which, I guess, was a good thing or you two would be girls."

"Huh?" Nicky said frowning.

"The Padstow curse! May no Padstow heir be born under the veil of protection. No male child has been born to the Padstow line in the valley since Godfrey. If your mum hadn't left the valley, which is protected by a spell to keep out anyone not borne inside the valley, you two would not have been born." said Auntie Lydia.

"So the "veil of protection" is the spell the villagers put over the valley?" asked Jamie.

"Yes dear!" said Auntie Amy. "Now to the day your parents disappeared. I had left for Europe a few days earlier and your aunt and uncle had gone into town to do a big grocery shop, which they do about once a month. Your mother had sent you two off to school and then went to do some shopping herself. While she was window-shopping on Oxford Street, she noticed a strange man watching her. We all have sixth sense when it comes to warlocks, she didn't think too much about it at first, then an hour later she saw the same man again, with another man, following her. She phoned your dad's office but was told that he hadn't turned up for work yet. She became scared because she had seen him off that morning and he hadn't said anything about going anywhere but to the office. She became even more scared when the two men were joined by a third. She didn't want to lead them back to you two, so she made a run for it. She managed to give them the slip on the underground, seems they didn't quite know how it works. She knew Ostrogoth had tried to get the crystal in the past and she was sure he was trying again. She was so scared for you two, she tried to contact us".

"Are you still talking about Ostrogoth, Cyrus Ostrogoth?" Jamie asked.

"Yes dear" answered Auntie Lydia.

"How can she get hold of you, you don't have a phone?" asked Nicky

Auntie Lydia got up, walked over to the sideboard, and picked up an unusual looking picture frame. It was round and flat, made of two pieces of glass pressed together, there was a photo of the three sisters between the glass. It stood on a wooden stand. She put it on the table and sat down.

"This is a Peekaboo. If I want to contact someone, all I do is this" and she tapped the glass three times and said, "Glass of sight, mist of might, bring forth Morton". The photo vanished in a swirling white mist and when it cleared, Uncle Morton's face was there.

"Can you bring home some pork chops for supper tonight dear?" she asked.

Uncle Morton's face smiled and said, "Of course, how about a nice roast for tomorrow as well?

"Yes, that would be lovely, thank you dear" she answered. She tapped it three more times, the mist engulfed Uncle Morton, and when it cleared, the photo was back.

"Wow! That's neat." Nicky said, picking up the picture and turning it over in his hands.

Auntie Amy continued. "Well, when she couldn't get hold of us or your dad she was very worried, she thought that Ostrogoth might have kidnapped all of us to force her to give him the crystal"

"Err…. Sorry, but how can Ostrogoth still be alive, he stole the crystal over 400 years ago?" Jamie interrupted again, not being able to get his head around the thought of Ostrogoth being the same one.

"Very well then." said Auntie Lydia, "Let's talk about Cyrus Ostrogoth. As you have probably found out, he dabbled in black magic when he was in the valley and was kicked out because he wouldn't stop. Well…. when he left, after stealing one of the crystals, he went off to Europe where, it is believed, he became very knowledgeable in the black arts, and, along with the crystal's rejuvenating powers and the black arts he has learned to prolong his life, he now wants the other crystal, to make him even more powerful and that could be devastating for the Specials…. he wants to wipe out white magic! He has a large following already and if he wipes out white magic, they will go after the Normals next."

"So it really IS the same guy?" said Jamie.

"For Christ's sake Jamie, get over it, there's more important things we need to know!" said Nicky irritably. "So you three were okay, but our dad, what happened to him?"

"We don't know sweetie, word has it that Ostrogoth has him and he's demanding the crystal, but we don't know where it is, even if we did, the village elders wouldn't let us give it to him because your dad's a Normal. " said Auntie Amy.

Nicky's face fell and he turned away,

"You mean the villagers wouldn't help?" Jamie looked from one to the other. "Isn't there some spell or something that can get him back, you know abracadabra and POW he's here?" Jamie hit the table with his fists and made everyone jump.

The aunts shook their heads. "The council is trying to come up with something. They have a lot of experience in this kind of thing."

"What about mum?" Nicky asked quietly.

"She's safe, I heard from her when I was in Europe, she's in hiding in a village up north, but she was very concerned about you two. I told her you were safe at a neighbour's, but she insisted we get you into the valley as quickly as possible."

"Why can't she come here too?" Nicky asked

"It's too dangerous for her to leave the village and you can't materialise or dematerialise here either," said Auntie Lydia.

"Materialise?" Jamie asked.

"It's how we travel, well, there's two ways actually, the most common way is with a pocket globe" Auntie Amy pulled a little round globe, about the size of a gobstopper, out of her pocket. It was attached to a chain with a key ring on the other end

"You put your finger on the area you want to go and it takes you to the nearest portal. The portal can be a Normals bus stop or a landmark of some kind or a building. The other way is more difficult but its more direct! You can actually appear within feet of your destination if you want." said Auntie Lydia, rising from the table and putting the kettle on for yet another cup of tea. She returned to the table saying, "So now you know, I guess there's no point in hiding anything else from you. Tomorrow I'll come to school with you and tell the headmaster that you have the gift and can stay all day!"

"What's that have to do with anything?" Jamie asked puzzled.

"Well, the reason you were sent home at lunchtime was because the other children had magic lessons in the afternoon, now you can start them too." she said.

The boys looked at each other, smiled and said sarcastically, "Great!"

The boys started magic lessons the very next afternoon and found them a lot of fun. They both proved to be very adept, the other children began talking to them and asking questions about growing up as Outside Normals. Then they spent most of the evening practicing spells and potions for homework, as well as the usual homework.

They saw very little of Charlotte during that week, except as a cat, but they did leave some homemade bread and jam at the top of the cellar stairs for her on one day and another day some left over roast beef and Yorkshire pudding. They were way too busy with homework to visit, but had left a note to say they would visit on the weekend and that in two weeks it would be Easter break [actually the Specials called it Spring Break it just happened to coincide with the Normals Easter break].

Chapter Ten

Constance Elder

"I've got to, at least try," said the tall, thin woman, pacing the floor as her curly red hair fell loosely around her shoulders

"But it's suicide Connie, you know it is!" replied the stout, older woman sitting at the kitchen table watching her friend pace.

"I know Roberta, but my boys, I miss them so much." Constance pleaded, tears beginning to fall from her green eyes.

"They're safe, they're with your sisters, no harm can come to them there." Roberta answered kindly.

"I know, I know, but I can't do anything here; at least there, with everyone, we have a chance to get Roger back!" Constance wiped the tears away defiantly with the sleeve of her shirt.

"I know it must be hard to be separated like this from your family but Roger will be okay as long as *HE* wants the crystal, he's not going to kill his only leverage." Roberta replied.

"I know everything you say is true, but I AM going and I need to know if you're going to help me or not?" Constance said resolutely.

"Well, you can't do it on your own, you need help so I guess I'm in." said Roberta unhappily.

"Thank you! At four then?" Constance said, more softly.

Constance left the kitchen to gather together the few possessions she'd collected while on the run and returned to the kitchen. The two women ate supper without talking and retired to bed early, Constance setting the alarm clock for half past three. She lay on the bed but couldn't sleep; her thoughts were of her boys she hadn't seen for almost a month. Then she thought about her husband, what they might be doing to him, they hated Normals. There were worse things than physical torture.

She went over and over her plan, not certain it would work but desperate to try. If they caught her they would be able to get into the valley, make her do anything they wanted, make her even kill her own children and sisters. Maybe she shouldn't try it, like Roberta said. But she had to, she needed to, she couldn't just sit here in safety. Roger needed her help and after all, she'd got him into this by marrying him. And the council hadn't been able to find him, they were a bunch of old fuddy duddy's, what good was a council with no power to stop warlocks?

She thought back to her father, who had fought almost all of his adult life to get more power for the council, after all, they were meant to be the Specials' Government. But for all his work, the Master Councillor had disbanded the Sorcerers because they hadn't heard anything of Ostrogoth for ten years so they assumed he was dead even though he hadn't been found. (The Sorcerers were a group of wizards who used the extreme magical arts to catch warlocks).

The alarm clock rang and she turned it off, she hadn't even closed her eyes! She got up, put on a tatty man's shirt, stuffed a pillow underneath it, and stepped into a pair of dirty overalls. She walked over to the mirror, tied up her unruly hair, reached down and picked up a grey wig, placed it over her hair, adjusted it, put an old straw hat on top of that and to complete the disguise, she placed a large grey moustache on her top lip. She looked at her reflection, nodded and left the room.

In the kitchen she found her friend dressed in a ragged old dress, a straw hat and Wellington boots. Together, they left the house and headed down the road in the cold, pre-dawn. Ahead villagers were preparing to take their produce to market…eggs, butter, cheese and organically grown fruits and vegetables… popular wares for the Market in the nearby town. Both ladies climbed aboard one of the wagons being pulled by a tractor, taking the last two seats in the already crowded wagon. The procession began to move towards the outskirts of the village, and then turned onto the road leading to the nearby town.

After a while, they passed a black car parked by the side of the road, with two men in it. *Obviously warlocks sent to keep an eye on everyone who travelled this road* Constance thought. They didn't do any more than stare at each face as the wagons passed. Fortunately for Constance, the sun had not yet risen, and with her back to the car, she looked like any other old farmer heading to market.

By the time they reached the town, the sky in the east was turning a pale winter grey. Everyone started setting up the stalls for market. Roberta dropped the green canvas sides down on one of the stalls and began helping an old lady place trays of eggs on the table. Constance slipped under the canvas side and stood behind the table, Roberta furtively glanced around looking for anything suspicious, then looked back at Constance and gave her a slight nod. Constance reached into her pocket and pulled out a very small globe, touched her finger to Cornwall and whispered, "Worldly wise ball, turn when I call and deliver me to Linton-On-Sea". The pocket globe began to spin in the palm of her hand, she just had enough time to say thank you to Roberta before she disappeared in a yellow flash.

A second later, there was another yellow flash and she appeared in a bus shelter on the outskirts of Linton-On-Sea. She dug into her pocket again and took out a small version of the Peekaboo.

She tapped it three times and said "Glass of sight, Mist of Light, Bring forth Lydia."

Lydia's sleepy face appeared on the glass, her eyes opened wide and she said, "Constance, where are you?"

"I'm at the bus stop in Linton, I daren't come any closer in case the valley is being watched, can you come and get me?" she replied, feeling very vulnerable.

"I'll meet you by the Monument, you should be able to see if anyone's coming and get out of there if you do, I'll be there with Morton in about half an hour."

The willowy mist returned and then the photo. She returned the Peekaboo to her pocket, looked around and, seeing no one about, headed away from town towards the rocky cliffs. Constance tried to walk like an old man, slightly bent over, but finding it hard to walk slowly with her heart racing, she pulled out the pillow, pulled off the moustache and wig and tossed them in a bush. She kept her hair tucked up inside the straw hat and carried on at a much faster pace, up the steep hill towards the Monument.

"Morton wake up, we have to go, oh!... for goodness sake Morton, wake up!" Lydia said, furiously shaking Morton awake,

He sprang out of bed. "Huh? What? Are you okay? What's going on?" he asked, scanning the shadowed corners for an intruder.

"Hurry, get dressed, Connie's at the Monument, we have to go and get her, don't just stand there, Morton hurry!" Lydia babbled.

Somehow, maybe because he had lived with her for years, he seemed to understand and within minutes, they were hurrying out into the chilly morning air to the garage. Morton started the car and was just pulling out when Amy came running out of the front door.

He stopped and said, "Stay here with the boys, we're going to get Connie, she's made it to the Monument" and the next second they were racing out of the driveway.

Amy stood there frozen to the spot, staring after the car with a million questions on her lips. What had made Constance risk her life to come here? Had she heard something about Roger?… had he got away or worse, had he been killed?

The chilly morning air penetrated her flannel pyjamas and she shivered. She turned and went back into the house, locking the usually unlocked door behind her. Amy couldn't go back to bed, her heart was pounding too fast and she had a terrible ache in the pit of her stomach. Absent-mindedly, she walked to the kitchen and put the kettle on. She looked up at the clock on the wall, the ornamental cat's eyes moved from side to side in time with its tail, as it ticked the minutes by; it was half past five, she calculated that it would take them approximately twenty five minutes to get to the Monument and then twenty five minutes back, giving ten minutes for unforeseeable events, they should be back in just over an hour.

The kettle boiled and she made herself a cup of tea, and the cats eyes kept moving back and forth as the minutes ticked slowly by.

* * * *

Constance, puffing from the walk up the steep hill, reached the Monument at twenty five past five; she had figured they should be there in ten, maybe fifteen minutes. She paced up and down in front of the grey monument trying to stay calm but alert. Behind the monument was the sea, so she didn't have to worry about that side, but in front were three paths leading to the monument, the one she had just come up, the one to the right came up at an angle from a parking lot at the bottom of the hill which was probably where Lydia would come, she thought, and one along the cliff edge which joined the path to the parking lot. This one was the easiest to see anyone coming along as there were no trees blocking her view, the parking lot was surrounded by trees and the path she came up also passed through trees so there wouldn't be a lot of warning if any warlocks came up those paths.

After a few minutes, she saw a lady walking a dog towards her along the cliff edge, She kept a close eye on the woman, thinking it was a little early to be walking a dog, but the lady crossed the grass and headed down the path Constance had come up and soon disappeared into the trees. She watched for a few more minutes and then let out a sigh of relief. Only five more minutes and they should be here.

Out of the corner of her eye, she thought she saw a flash from a car's headlight through the trees by the parking lot. She watched but no car came into view so she turned to look down the path she had come up; it was clear. She looked along the cliff path; it was clear too. Glancing back towards the parking lot, she let out an involuntary scream, two men were running up the path towards her! She fumbled in her pocket for the globe, it was stuck, she glanced back at the men, they would be on top of her in seconds, she started to run down the path in front of her, suddenly there was another flash and another man appeared at the bottom of the path, she turned, cut across the grass and headed to the cliff path, trying all the time to get the globe out of her pocket.

Finally Constance managed to free the pocket globe but she was running too fast to keep her finger in one spot, she could hear the men gaining on her, she couldn't stop, she headed down the hill towards the trees, she hoped she might be able to lose them in there.

Reaching the trees, she darted between them, jumping over the undergrowth, glancing over her shoulder at every opportunity. She saw the closest man fall, hoping he had lost sight of her, she threw herself down among the dewy ferns and, began crawling along under them, she came to a stop and lay pressed against the roots of a tree with the ferns covering her, she held her breath but her heart was pounding so loud she felt sure the men following would hear it.

"Did you see where she went?" asked one of the warlocks.

Another said, "I thought you were right behind her!"

"Yeah, well I tripped and lost her, didn't I?" said the first.

"Well we'd better find her or you know what'll happen" said another.

Constance lay motionless listening to them moving through the trees, hitting the ferns with sticks; one was getting closer and closer, she could see his mean face through the ferns, any minute he would step on her if he didn't see her first.

A man's voice, which she thought she recognised, yelled "Over here!" and the men ran off in the other direction. Constance lay there forcing herself to breathe easier, listening to the men get further and further away, when suddenly a hand was over her mouth! She tried to scream but couldn't and a soft voice said, "Shhhhh!!"

The hand moved from her mouth; she spun around. Morton was kneeling behind her, smiling. He beckoned her to follow him and they crept on all fours among the undergrowth until they reach the middle path. Morton popped his head out and then scooted over to the other side of the path, he beckoned Constance to follow and they ran for the parking lot as quickly and quietly as they could. At the edge of the woods Constance saw the old station wagon with its engine running and the back door open. Lydia was standing by the door keeping watch. She beckoned to Constance, Constance ran for the car and leapt into the back, Lydia quickly threw a blanket over her and slammed the door.

Morton was already behind the wheel as Lydia jumped into the passenger seat and they took off like a bat out of hell. He looked in the rear view mirror and saw a couple of flashes, he knew the men had de-materialised. They sped down the country lanes at 80 miles an hour, flew around corners and over the last hill only to find, just a few hundred yards from the entrance to the valley, two black cars blocking the road. Morton took a quick right down another road and pulled over.

"Now what are we going to do?" Morton asked.

"We need a diversion" Lydia answered and, reaching into her pocket she took out a Peekaboo. She called for Amy and when Amy's distraught face appeared, Lydia said, "Pull yourself together Amy, I need you to round up the troops and send them to the entrance, it's being blocked by two black cars and we can't get in".

"Okay, they'll be there in a few minutes. Have you got her?" said Amy, tears now running down her face. Lydia nodded.

Morton, in the meantime, had turned the car around and parked just close enough to the crossroads for him to see the cars and they waited.

Constance poked her head out from under the blanket. "How do they know where the entrance is?" she asked.

"I'm not sure they do, they just know it's on this road somewhere!" answered Lydia

"Lucky guess then huh?" said Constance, and Lydia nodded.

Before long they could hear an argument developing. Morton craned his neck to see three cars loaded with Specials from the valley trying to get past the two black cars. Mr. Pennith was yelling at the warlocks and before the warlocks knew what hit them a Spell was cast on them and then they were thrown into the boot of their own cars. Two of the Specials then jumped into the warlocks' cars and drove away leaving the road clear.

Morton stepped on the gas and sped towards the dirt road. He took the corner at an unbelievable speed but made it into the valley where he slowed down and soon found himself being followed by two of the vehicles from the valley. They were safe!

The station wagon turned slowly into the driveway of the mansion and a few seconds later pulled up in front of the stables. Three very weary people stepped out and headed towards the kitchen door. It was flung open and a crying Amy grabbed Constance in a bear like hug sobbing,

"Connie, Connie, you're safe, you're here!" then she threw her back at arms length, said

"Are you nuts?" and again hugged her.

The kettle boiled in the kitchen and, with Amy in no fit state, Morton made the tea while Amy sobbed and then yelled and held onto Constance as if she thought she was going to disappear.

Finally Constance extricated herself from Amy's embrace and asked, "Where's my boys?"

"On the third floor, red and blue rooms." Lydia answered softly.

Constance, feeling exhausted and barely able to move, slowly walked out of the kitchen and climbed unsteadily up to the third floor. She felt as if she had run a marathon, her legs were like jelly, but she forced herself on, she needed to see her boys! She quietly opened Nicky's door and slipped inside. Dawn was just breaking, but it was still very dark in his room. She could here his soft snoring from the other side of the room; she let her eyes adjust to the dark and tiptoed over to the bed.

Constance looked down at the curly red hair and cherub-like face poking out from under the covers; she gently stroked his cheek and then leant over and kissed his forehead. She wanted so badly to hug him, hold him, and see that smile, a smile only a child can give their mother. She bent down and kissed him again. A teardrop fell onto his cheek and a sleepy voice said, "Mum?" Constance looked down into deep brown eyes that were trying to focus on her face in the dark.

"Yes, munchkin it's me, I'm home!" Constance said softly.

Suddenly, Nicky's arms were around her neck, yelling, "Mum you're here, you're really here, I've missed you so much, oh mum I can't believe you're here!"

A light went on in the other room and Jamie yelled, "What's wrong, are you having another bad dream?"

Nicky yelled back, "It's mum Jamie, mum's here!"

There was the sound of stumbling feet, the door was flung wide and Jamie came stampeding into the room. He jumped across the bed and threw himself into his mother's embrace. Both boys hung onto her so tightly she could hardly breath but she didn't mind, she had waited a long time to be hugged by her boys and nothing mattered anymore but this moment, a moment she wanted never to end. All three were crying and Jamie could hear her sobbing voice saying softly, "My boys, I love you so much, if anything had happened to you I wouldn't have been able to go on! Being apart from you was more than I could bear!"

Chapter Eleven

Preparations

The morning light crept slowly into the kitchen but the three occupants sitting at the table in lively conversation didn't notice. The boys, still in their pyjamas, had been telling their mum everything that had happened since arriving in the village except, of course, about Charlotte; and she had been telling them everything she had been through since the morning she disappeared.

"....... and then this hand went around my mouth, I thought I was going to have a heart attack..... Oh! Is that the time?" Constance said, turning around as the door opened and glancing up at the clock.

"Go on, what happened then?" Jamie said, excitedly.

"Well it was your Uncle Morton, how he found me, I don't know, but I was never more happy to see anyone in my life".

"What happened to the Warlocks?" Nicky asked, his brown eyes the size of saucers.

"Well I'm not quite sure…"

"They headed off in the other direction, I was worried they would spot me, so I hid behind the car." Lydia chirped in as she filled the kettle for tea.

"Then what?" asked Jamie.

"We jumped in the car and tore out of there, I didn't know that old station-wagon of mine could go so fast, but the Warlocks beat us here or else managed to get a message to the couple at the entrance, but the Pennith's and a couple of others soon took care of them." Uncle Morton said, smiling.

"Our teachers?" Nicky said shocked.

"Yes dear, we're a very small community and everyone helps everyone, especially when it comes to Warlocks!" said Auntie Lydia.`

The six of them sat around the table talking happily and eating breakfast until Uncle Morton suddenly jumped up and said,

"Oh dear, I'm late for work and you two are going to be late for school."

"I'll send a message to the Pennith's to let them know the boys won't be in today, shall I Connie?" Lydia asked. Connie nodded gratefully, the thought of sending the boys off to school and spending a couple of hours away from them so soon was not something she wanted to do right now.

Nicky got up to fill the kettle with water for yet another cup of tea and noticed the tabby cat sitting in the courtyard. He put the kettle on the stove, poured some milk into a bowl, and slipped out of the kitchen door. He put the milk down just outside the kitchen door, followed the cat out of sight of the kitchen window, and waited for her to change. When Charlotte had transformed, he started babbling excitedly. She put her hands on his shoulders and he calmed down.

"Sorry, I'm just so excited, my mum's come back, she arrived this morning, she nearly got caught but she got away!" Nicky babbled, his brown eyes sparkling.

"Yes, I heard the commotion this morning when I was out hunting, I wondered what had happened, that's wonderful news!" Charlotte said, "You had better get back before they miss you. But come and see me later, we have lots to do if we're going to rescue your father?" and before Nicky had chance to ask what she meant, Jamie opened the kitchen door and said,

"What are you doing out here, mum's getting worried?"

"Sorry, just giving the cat some milk." Nicky said, and Jamie knew he meant he was talking to Charlotte, but when Nicky turned to finish his conversation with Charlotte, she was gone.

The boys walked back inside and found the sisters discussing bedroom arrangements.

"I would much prefer to be on the third floor with the boys Lydia." Constance was saying.

"But those rooms haven't been used for years, they're under dustcovers and your room's been kept just as you left it!" Lydia said impatiently.

"Don't worry, the boys and I will clean it up, you do enough around here without worrying about a room for me, anyway my old room is too far away from the boys and I've spent enough time away from them already. You'll help me clean the room, won't you boys?" said Constance smiling at the boys.

"We'd love to, we've learnt quite a lot of spells and potions at school that will help make the room look brand new," they said excitedly.

Lydia didn't seem too impressed by the thought of them using spells and potions that they had only just learnt, but Constance said with a chuckle, "I'll keep a check on their enthusiasm."

"I have some clothes that might fit you." Lydia said, looking at Constance's dirty disguise.

"Thanks, I guess I'm going to have to get hold of some more clothes somewhere," said Constance.

"You're not planning on leaving the valley, are you?" said her frightened sisters.

"No of course not, the Milliners must have some clothes," she answered, smiling at the shocked faces.

"The Milliners have some stuff but not the London fashions you're used to." said Amy.

"That's okay, I just need some basic clothes, you know, jeans and sweaters and a couple of pairs of socks." Constance replied.

Constance and Lydia went up to Lydia's room to check her closet. They found a skirt with an elastic waist, which was good as Lydia was shorter and plumper than Constance; a baggy sweater, a pair of socks and a pair of runners. As Constance was changing, Lydia said,

"I did try to keep the boys away from it you know, I knew you didn't want them knowing any of our ways."

"I know, the boys told me that they discovered it on their own, in fact they had to confront you and Amy and show you what they had learnt before you would admit to anything." Constance said laughing, " I would've loved to see your faces at that moment. Anyway, it wasn't me it was Roger, he thought that if they didn't know anything, they would be safe".

While Constance and Lydia were finding some clothes, the boys went upstairs to get the cleaning supplies together. Constance soon joined them and, after checking out both rooms, decided on the room closest to the bathroom, as this one seemed to be in better shape than the other. Nicky pulled back the thick, green velvet curtains at the windows and began removing the dust-covers, but he was making so much dust, his mother told him to stop. She beckoned him to stand next to her, peered out of the door to make sure the corridor was clear, winked at him and said,

> "Lonely, forgotten room so cold,
> Shake off the dust, dirt and mould,
> Be bright, sunny, fresh and gay,
> If you wish for me to stay."

She waved her hand gently through the air. The thick layer of dust changed to shimmering particles, slowly rising into the air and finally exploding like little fireworks, leaving the room completely dust free.

"Wow! that was great, how'd you do that?" Nicky asked, his eyes sparkling with enthusiasm.

Constance laughed. "That was one of the first spells I learnt when I was a girl, I hated cleaning my room. But don't tell your aunts, they get very mad at me when I take short-cuts".

Jamie poked his head in and said, "I've found the potion we can use on the furniture…" his mouth dropped open, as he looked around the room "….what happened, how did you clean it up so quickly?"

Nicky whispered, "Mum knows a neat spell for cleaning up rooms."

"Can you teach us?" Jamie asked with a twinkle in his eyes.

Constance laughed again and agreed.

Jamie had been longing to try the potion for restoring old furniture ever since Nicky had pointed it out in the book. So he said he was going to find the worst piece of furniture in the room, so he chose a very old, battered dresser, he put some polish onto the cloth Amy had given him and started to rub it all over the dresser, he then buffed vigorously. First the small scratches disappeared, then the deeper ones and finally the really deep gouges. He stood back and admired his work; he couldn't believe that it was the same piece of furniture.

He polished a couple more pieces of furniture until his mum asked if he would take the rug downstairs and beat it, as they had to make it look like they had cleaned the room. He picked up the rug with Nicky's help and together they carried it downstairs. When they reached the courtyard where the washing line was, they threw the rug over and Jamie began beating the carpet. A voice behind them said, "You two look busy!".

They turned to see the tabby cat sitting close behind them.

"Yeah, we're helping mum clean up her room." Nicky said.

"We need to get together soon if we're going to help your father before it's too late, when do you think you can get away?" said the cat.

"How can we help dad?" asked Jamie.

"I've had years to read lots of books and to practice as well as learn some defences against black magic," said the cat.

"Okay, we'll try and get away after lunch, should we meet in the cellar or at the summerhouse?" asked Jamie.

"The summerhouse! I haven't been in there for a hundred years!" said the cat.

The boys went back to beating the rug. Then took it back upstairs to find Constance standing in the doorway admiring the spotless room. What a transformation! They now noticed the pale yellow wallpaper, a pattern of green vines intertwined with big pink and yellow flowers covered the walls, the room was a lot brighter now that the curtains were drawn back and the light could come in. The four poster bed, which had been lovingly restored by Jamie, had had the velvet curtains removed at Constance's insistence, was now made up with fresh sheets and a big fluffy quilt covered in small pink flowers trimmed in green which Lydia had brought up. The fireplace was clean and a roaring fire was now removing the dampness from the room. Every piece of furniture sparkled unnaturally and the smell of lemon polish hung in the air. Crocheted doilies sat on most surfaces with family photos standing upon them.

Nicky ran off to his room, returning a few seconds later carrying a vase of beautiful flowers.

"I changed these from dried flowers and I think they will look perfect right here, don't you mum?"

She walked over and gave him a hug and nodded, he placed the flowers on a small table in front of the window. They unrolled the rug and replaced the armchairs in front of the fire. The room looked perfect.

* * * *

After lunch the boys asked if they could go for a walk, which Constance, reluctantly, agreed to. They left, as usual, by the kitchen door, crossed the lawn and soon were at the summerhouse. Charlotte hadn't yet arrived so they opened up the window and climbed inside, leaving the window open for Charlotte. The summerhouse looked quite cosy now that the boys had cleaned it up and fixed the broken furniture.

The tabby cat jumped through the window a few minutes later and transformed. Charlotte's eyes took in every familiar detail of the summerhouse and tears glistened in her eyes. The boys didn't say anything, feeling a little uncomfortable, knowing that this had been a special place for her and that her father had taken it away, they just watched as she walked around touching a table and the back of a chair, then she looked up at the portrait of herself; she stared at it for sometime, the boys couldn't make out what she was thinking. After a while she turned and sat down on the couch next to Nicky, wiping tears from her eyes on a lace hanky.

The boys looked at her expectantly and they weren't disappointed. By the time they had returned to the manor, they had formulated a plan. All they had to do was practice some Defences from a book that Charlotte had told them to get out of the Library, after that, go and rescue their dad. But it wasn't going to be that easy, of course! Their first attempt at Defences wasn't successful; also they had no idea where their father was. At the moment though, they were oblivious to these obstacles, but very shortly it would become all too clear.

The rest of the week passed as usual, school, lunch, school, homework, supper, family time, bed. But they spent an hour practicing Defences before they finally got to bed. At ten o'clock, just before retiring herself, Constance would come into their rooms to give them a final kiss goodnight, not realising that they had probably only just jumped into bed. At half past ten, they would sneak off down to the cellar to spend an hour with Charlotte, correcting the problems they had encountered.

Charlotte had taught them the "Stupifying Spell", which rendered a person unable to think clearly. The "Counter-Spell Spell" which stopped spells from touching them and was trying to teach them the "Invisibility Spell", which would help them get past a lot of warlocks at one time.

The boys were working so hard to master these spells that they were staying up later and later, and now, Mrs. Pennith had noticed Nicky almost falling asleep in her class. As the other children ran off at playtime she called him to her desk and asked,

"I noticed you were almost asleep through history yesterday and again today you were falling asleep in English, would you like to tell me what's wrong?"

"Nothing's wrong, I'm just tired that's all!" Nicky said, stifling a yawn.

"Yes, I can tell you're tired Nicky, but why are you?" she persisted

"I've been staying up too late doing my homework, I guess" Nicky said, kicking an invisible piece of dirt.

"Why have you been leaving your homework so late?" she asked.

Nicky shrugged his shoulders.

"I know it must be hard, to concentrate on homework when you have the worry of your father, but people are working to get him back", she said kindly.

"Oh! we're going to get him back!" Nicky said without thinking.

"Well that's a very good attitude to have, but it doesn't explain why you're staying up late doing your homework", she said.

"Oh well... um... we want to get it right!" Nicky mumbled, feeling confused.

"Nicky, are you and your brother planning something?" It was Mrs. Pennith's turn to feel confused.

"No, oh no…err.. we just want to get everything right…. that's all!" Nicky said unconvincingly.

She studied his face, knowing he was hiding something and finally she said,

"Okay you can go, but I want to see ALL that homework you've been doing and if it doesn't measure up, I will be contacting your mother".

Nicky ran out of the classroom, thankful that he hadn't let the cat out of the bag! He met Jamie and told him what had happened.

"She's bound to tell mum when you don't produce the homework, why did you have to say that to a teacher of all people?" said Jamie angrily.

"I don't know, she got me flustered!" Nicky replied, sulkily.

"I know, we'll ask Charlotte for an easy spell book and you can practice some easy stuff to show her and maybe she won't tell mum". Nicky nodded feeling only slightly relieved.

Even though Jamie was three years older than the other children in Nicky's class, Jamie had Magic Lessons with them. Nicky and Jamie couldn't believe that all the kids found it so normal and would complain about having to do certain things, such as potions, whereas Nicky and Jamie couldn't wait for the afternoon classes and this afternoon was no exception. They were learning how to make a healing potion. The school was providing the ingredients, which included some very weird sounding things, so the class had to be very careful not to spill any. They also learnt that measuring precisely was of the utmost importance. When a chubby little boy, name Cecil, at the back of the class, added a tablespoon of Ground Unicorn Horn instead of a teaspoon and ended up removing another boy's nose as well as the pimple upon it. Luckily Mrs. Pennith had a "counter-potion" to fix anything and the boy's nose soon returned.

Nicky had made friends with a girl named Caliandra, Cali for short, who sat next to him in class; she was the same girl who had smiled at him on their first day. She had helped him one afternoon when his potion started to boil over. Cali had told him that her parents had said she was to stay away from him because Ostrogoth wouldn't stop at just kidnapping their Dad; he would probably go after them too, to get what he wanted. But she told Nicky that she didn't think that that was right, and instead, everyone in the village should be helping them, not turning their backs on them; this had made them fast friends.

Cali was very pretty, with dark hair, enormous brown eyes surrounded by thick black eyelashes, and she was very athletic. She played on the boys' football team, she also did gymnastics and wanted to try out for the Olympics but her parents said she couldn't because she was a witch.

Most playtimes, she would join Nicky and Jamie as they walked around the playground, discussing their plans to get their Dad back. At first she tried to discourage them, telling them that Ostrogoth was way too powerful for them, and even for anyone who had grown up learning magic; but when she realised that she wasn't going to talk them out of it, she decided her best bet was to help them any way she could. She had told them that her dad worked for the Council and she would pass on any information she overheard concerning Ostrogoth and his whereabouts.

This particular playtime, she joined them to find out what Mrs. Pennith had wanted, Nicky told her, as she walked with them.

She said, "She will tell your mum, but it will be out of concern, not out of spite she's a good teacher even though she's strict and if she thinks you're up to something....."

"It's okay, we've decided what we're going to do. I think we can fool her!" said Jamie confidently. Cali looked at Nicky's frown and asked,

"What's wrong?"

"If I don't fool her and she tells Mum.....I don't like lying to her, anyway she always catches me and then she gets that look in her eyes and I feel horrible", Nicky answered.

"Don't worry, she won't find out as long as you do a good job on those spells and we'll have Dad home and she'll be so happy, she won't even remember we lied to her", Jamie replied, cockily.

But Nicky wasn't so confident anymore; it had stopped being a game a while ago. Now all he felt was tired and scared and Jamie wouldn't listen to his doubts; all Jamie could see was the look on his mum's face when be brought his dad home to her! Jamie would be a hero!

Somehow, he had to get through to Jamie that this wasn't a game, this was real!

Chapter Twelve

Where is Roger Elder?

Where is Roger Elder? That was the question everyone was asking; even now the Normals Police Force was scouring the whole of Britain looking for him. No word had come since the morning he disappeared. At first the Police thought it was a domestic dispute and Roger had done something to Constance, but now Constance had been found and had told the police as much, and as little as she could, so they were treating Roger's disappearance as a kidnapping. But as far as the police knew, there hadn't been a ransom! The Council couldn't tell them about Ostrogoth, that he was holding Roger and the ransom he was demanding was the Crystal. If the Council had had their way the Police would never have been contacted in the first place, but the Stirlings didn't know any of this either and they had called them, out of concern for Jamie and Nicky.

The Council also knew that, if they handed over the Crystal, always supposing they could find it, Roger would almost certainly be killed because he wouldn't be of any use anymore. This they had told to Constance, Lydia, Morton and Amy and they'd all agreed that the longer they stalled, the more chances they would have of finding him. But no one had found even a hint of where Ostrogoth was, no unexplained deaths or disappearances, no flocks of birds falling out of the sky for no apparent reason... nothing!

Finally, the Council had called back into service, some of the Sorcerers who had been hunting Ostrogoth. The Sorcerers had set out in different directions, following leads they had found before they were disbanded. But the leads were years old and most went nowhere. However, one lead looked promising; Milton Blueblood had the best record for capturing warlocks. He was following a lead in Scotland, actually a small island off Scotland, which seemed to appear and disappear. He had set off as soon as he had been reinstated and the sketchy reports he sent back were promising.

Cali had overheard her father telling her mother about Milton Blueblood and was now informing Jamie and Nicky.

"He said that Milton Blueblood was already on the coast of Scotland, interviewing fishermen, some told him that this island suddenly appeared right in the middle of their fishing ground. It would get very misty and when the mist cleared, this island would be there!"

"So your dad thinks this is Ostrogoth, he somehow manages to materialise a whole island?" Jamie was thunderstruck.

"Yeah, he's very powerful; they say he can kill you with a stare", Cali answered.

Jamie was finally beginning to realise this was serious stuff; it wasn't a game and he began to have doubts that Nicky and he could get their dad back on their own.

"How many warlocks does your dad think are with him?" Jamie asked.

"He doesn't know for sure but some say he has thousands, they're not all with him, they're spread out doing jobs for him, probably twenty to thirty are with him right now"

"Phew.... I didn't think it would be that many, how are we supposed to get past that many?" Jamie asked.

"I think we should talk to Charlotte, she can't know he's that strong!" Nicky said, forgetting that Cali didn't know about Charlotte.

"Who's Charlotte?" asked Cali.

Jamie gave Nicky a dirty look and hit him on the arm.

"Ouch, that hurt, I forgot okay?" Nicky said angrily.

"Well, who's Charlotte?" asked Cali again.

"She's a secret and if we tell you, you must promise not to tell anyone" Jamie said.

"I promise!", she said, raising her hand and crossing her heart.

"Charlotte is Charlotte Whitehaven, have you heard of her?" asked Nicky.

"Yeah, she was murdered by her dad when she was about sixteen, my dad told me the story his dad told him, how can she be still alive, she would be 200 years old?"

"Well, she's not THAT old.... a hundred and something, she escaped from the north turret...." and Jamie told her the whole story and how Nicky had found her and everything else.

"Wow, so she's been helping you learn Defences, and she thinks you two alone can save your dad where the Council and Sorcerers can't, she must be crazy or senile", she scoffed.

"No she's not, I just don't think she realises how strong he really is, she doesn't have much contact with people. Would you like to meet her?" Nicky asked.

"Yeah I'd love to!", Cali replied eagerly.

"I'll check with her and make arrangements, if it's okay!", Nicky said.

* * * *

"Why did you tell her, you promised me you wouldn't tell anyone," Charlotte said unhappily

"I'm really, really sorry, I didn't mean to, it just slipped out, you'll like her, she's really nice and she's promised not to tell anyone, will you p-l-e-a-s-e meet her?" Nicky pleaded.

"Alright, after school, I'll meet you in the graveyard." She sounded really upset.

Nicky had taken some milk outside so he could talk to Charlotte; she was so upset by his betrayal, even though it was accidental, that she hadn't even bothered to turn back into a cat when she left him. Nicky felt awful, the last thing he wanted to do was upset Charlotte, she had helped them so much. He wondered how he could make it up to her. Then it came to him and he ran off towards the vegetable garden. Fifteen minutes later he slipped into the Conservatory through the open door and tiptoed to the Library, hurried over to the bookcase, opened it, slid behind it and gently pulled the bookcase closed. He lit the lamp at the top and quietly descended the dank cold steps; he reached the bottom and headed for Charlotte's chamber.

Charlotte wasn't there when he arrived, so he started looking for somewhere to put it. That was it! The perfect place. Charlotte arrived a few minutes later and transformed in the outer chamber. When she entered, she saw Nicky, then her eyes travelled up above the fireplace, she put her hands over her mouth and started to cry. Nicky felt really bad now, he didn't want to make her cry, he was trying to make her feel better.

"I'm sorry, I'll take it back, please don't cry!", he begged.

"No, no, Nicky you didn't do anything wrong, you're a sweet boy for doing this for me, thank you!" she cried with happiness.

Nicky looked confused, but Charlotte was still staring above the fireplace. There hung her portrait, the portrait she hadn't seen for a hundred years, except when she went to the summerhouse a few days ago, and now this dear, sweet boy had brought it here for her. She walked over and hugged him.

The following day after school, and the beginning of Spring Break, the boys and Cali headed to the graveyard. It only took a few minutes to get there and when they walked over to the bench to wait, they saw the grey tabby cat coming towards them. Cali didn't pay any attention to her but the boys did. When she got to them, she sat down in front of Cali and stared at her. At first Cali paid no attention to her but the staring began to bother her.

"What's wrong with that stupid cat?"

"That's rather rude, isn't it?" said the cat.

Cali, startled, jumped onto the bench, staring at the cat with her mouth wide open. The boys began to laugh, then Charlotte transformed and Cali started to laugh too, stepping down from the bench. Charlotte was smiling and said,

"Do you know how many times I've wanted to do that to people?" and they all started to laugh again.

Charlotte accepted Cali into their little group and suggested she help the boys learn some new spells. Jamie decided that this was a good time to tell Charlotte that he thought they were in way over their heads.

"You have to believe in yourselves, boys, you can do this!" she replied.

"But he's so powerful and has loads of followers" Jamie said.

"He can move an island!", Nicky chirped in.

"He's powerful yes, but you two can be more powerful because you have Padstow blood running through your veins and you have the power of the Crystal!", she answered.

"But he has the other Crystal" Nicky reminded her.

"Yes but the Crystals were meant for good and when good is near, the power transfers to the good. He will not be able to use the Crystal against you, but it will give you more power. You must believe in yourselves, just like John Padstow, do you think John Padstow would have found the Crystals if the Crystals didn't see good in him? Ostrogoth may have stolen one of them and used it for evil, but it has taken a terrible toll on him, he has had to use all the black arts he knows to keep it with him and they say he fights with it every day to stop it over-powering a weaker mind".

"So why didn't he just throw it away?" Jamie asked logically.

"Because he believes he's greater than the Crystal and is determined to use it for evil, he still wants to destroy the valley and, in his mind, the only way to do that is to use the Crystals.

Why else would he insist on the other Crystal? In his warped mind, he thinks that if he has both Crystals, the valley will fall".

"Yes but, doesn't that mean that if he gets anywhere near the valley, any good witch will be able to control the Crystals?" said Nicky.

"Yes, but I doubt if he is planning on coming anywhere near the valley, not with Padstow blood still here; he will use the Crystal and the black arts from a distance, to prevent a Padstow from gaining control."

"Is it just Padstows that control the Crystals?" asked Jamie.

"The correct term is use the Crystals, no one can control them and yes, you are right, the Padstows have a strong connection to them and they work best with Padstows, but other witches have been known to use them."

Cali listened to Charlotte and realised why the boys believed everything she said. She had an aura about her that was overwhelming, she felt it herself. She wasn't too sure that Charlotte was right about the Crystals but she was sure going to find out before her friends did anything stupid, like go up against Ostrogoth.

Cali said, "I'd better go before mum comes looking for me," and ran off.

Charlotte transformed back into the cat and walked home with the boys.

That evening, sitting at the dining table in the Pendoggett's small, but neat dining room, Cali listened, without showing any sign of paying any attention, as her dad related the day's news to her mum,

"Blueblood finally got another report to us, turns out he was right, the island is how Ostrogoth's been able to stay hidden all these years. He somehow learnt to dematerialise the whole island. That makes him more powerful than anyone we have on our side, not even Blueblood himself thinks he can take him down". He put another bite of apple pie in his mouth and continued. "Blueblood extracted the information from one of Ostrogoth's warlocks with a truth spell; he also found out that Roger Elder is being held in the dungeons of the castle on the island. He's not heavily guarded but it's almost impossible to get onto the island because Ostrogoth has so many protection spells placed on it." He wagged his spoon in her direction and little pieces of pie flew onto the table, Cali's mum cringed as she watched them land on her nice shiny table "We are going to have to do a lot of strategy planning to launch any kind of rescue."

"Won't he know someone's found him if one of his follower's is missing?" Cali's mum asked taking her eyes away from the crumbs.

"No, Blueblood assured me that he cleared the warlock's mind and of course, he has that ability of his." said Cali's dad.

"Dad?" Cali said, casually, taking advantage of the lull in conversation.

"Yes, honey?" he answered.

"You know the Padstow Crystals?" Her dad nodded. "The one Ostrogoth's got, if good is near, will it give power to that person or will Ostrogoth still be able to use it?".

"What made you think of that honey?" asked Cali's mum.

"Oh, we were talking about the Crystals at school today in history, and one of those boys asked the teacher", she lied.

"As far as history tells us, if someone good were standing face to face with someone bad, the power will go to the good side.", he replied.

"Is it true that they work better for a Padstow than anyone else?"

"That's what they say, but the crystals have been missing for longer than I've been alive, so it would be hard to prove", he said.

"But if it can choose good over evil, why would it work at all for someone evil?"

"Well it doesn't have a mind to actually choose, but there's a lot of things in this world that are hard to explain and these crystals are one of them, history tells us that when John Padstow found the Crystals he was lead there by a hawk, some think the hawk somehow gave the Crystals their power and others think the Crystals are unique in that nature gave them the power of healing and with the powers of the Specials it amplifies that power." He smiled indulgently at his daughter.

"Thanks Dad, they really should teach that in school, I had no idea how special the Crystals are. …. Err.. Mum…. those boys… Nicky and Jamie… you know they're now in afternoon classes with us and they're picking it up really easily…. Mrs. Pennith says they have the Padstow gift. Well, I was thinking that, now that they're one of us, would it be alright if I made friends with them now?" Cali asked hopefully.

"What you're really saying is, you've already made friends with them and want me to say its okay right?"

Cali nodded sheepishly.

"I have my concerns about their safety but I've know their mother all my life and if they are as gifted as she is, and they know our secret, I can't see any harm in it; okay?" Cali's mum said smiling.

Cali threw her arms around her mum's neck, kissed her on the cheek and said, "Thanks Mum, you're the best!"

"But remember Cali, they haven't grown up here like you have and they are not going to understand all our ways, so it will be up to you to curb their enthusiasm and we don't want the Normals discovering us. They may be descendents of the Padstows but they were raised as Normals, they can't possibly understand what the Specials have gone through." said her father, sternly.

The next morning, even though it was Saturday, Cali woke up early and, after having a quick breakfast, she called Nicky on the Peekaboo, she told him she had some information and asked if she could come over. Nicky said he'd meet her at the gate.

Cali lived with her parents in one of the newer cottages on the school road and it only took her five minutes to get there. As they walked down the service road to the courtyard, Cali told him what her father had said, which made Nicky even more worried about their ability to get their father back. He said he'd have to find Jamie and tell him. They found Jamie sitting on the wall of the veranda drinking lemonade and watching the sheep grazing in the field. They sat down and Cali repeated what she had heard. The boys decided they were going to have to talk to Charlotte one more time.

Nicky noticed the grey tabby sitting on the fence post completely still, he assumed she was hunting again and pointed her out. They got up and headed towards her across the lawn. As they approached, she turned to look at them, jumped down and walked towards the woods. They followed her and by the time they caught up with her, she had transformed.

"Why are you still hunting, don't we bring you enough meat?" Nicky asked.

"Yes dear, but it's a cat's nature to hunt and I've been doing it for so long now" she said.

"We need to talk to you," Jamie said "Cali has heard something that we think you should hear"

Cali repeated what her father had said for the third time and they waited for Charlotte to respond. She looked away towards the sea for quite some time and when she looked back she said,

"I guess you feel you're not up to the task, maybe I was wrong about you two, if you had been raised in the valley you wouldn't think twice about going after your father. But you're still thinking like Normals, you just see the numbers and say you can't do it. It's not the numbers, it's the power and good always triumphs over evil"

"That's not fair!" Jamie said indignantly, "We've only learnt three spells and we're not very good at those, he's had 400 years to practice the black arts, how's two boys with less than a month's practice and three spells, going to defeat him?"

"You're looking at it all wrong, you don't have to defeat him, that's what he's expecting. No, you only have to sneak in, deal with a few warlocks that are guarding your father and get out. Master the invisibility spell and you will be able to get on the island easily." Charlotte said.

"It's getting off the island that bothers me" Jamie said

"And what about all the other spells he's supposed to have and all those warlocks?" Nicky piped in.

"One step at a time." Charlotte said calmly.

No one said anything for a long time. Charlotte changed and went back to her hunting and the three of them stood watching her. Cali broke the silence by saying,

"Show me what you've learned"

"Okay but we need to go to our rooms for powder. Come on!" Nicky replied and they walked off across the lawns towards the mansion.

In Nicky's bedroom they opened the secret door and removed the spell books and the velvet drawstring bags. Nicky faced Jamie, took out some dust from one of the bags, said, "Stupefacere", and blew dust at Jamie.

Jamie yelled, "Contra Spellam" and raised his hands, as a flash of yellowy-green light was about to hit his head, it bounced off of his hands and dissipated.

"That's very good, but have you tried the Stupefying Spell on someone and seen its effects, if you don't do it very well, it only lasts a few seconds instead of hours and have you tried the Counter-spell against the black arts?" Cali asked.

Both boys shook their heads and Jamie asked, "Who are we meant to practice on?"

And Nicky said, "Who knows the black arts and would be willing to use them?"

Cali smiled knowingly and said "There's a couple of warlocks at the entrance to the valley so my dad says, he's warned everyone not to go out. I bet they wouldn't mind using the black arts."

"Maybe we should practice the Invisibility Spell first and get that right, then we could use that to sneak up on them", Nicky said.

They all agreed. Jamie went first. "Vail of light, Shroud of might, Hide me from their sight."

He sprinkled some elf dust over himself. The dust fell gently and dissolved, slowly his head started to become transparent and disappeared, then his shoulders and his torso and down his legs BUT his feet were still solid and they stayed solid. Nicky and Cali started to laugh. But Jamie didn't find it funny and shouted, "Vail of light, Shroud of might, bring me back to sight."

And he reappeared. Nicky went next, but he used too much elf dust and couldn't bring himself back for fifteen minutes. Cali tried and got it perfect, no feet sticking out and no problem returning. So the boys tried again and again and again. They practiced for almost two hours, until they heard their mother calling them from the bottom of the third floor stairs for lunch.

The three of them ran down and caught up with Constance going down the grand staircase.

"So who's this?" Constance asked with surprise seeing Cali.

"This is Cali, we met at school" Nicky answered, "She's been helping us with our homework"

Constance gave them a funny look and said, "I'm assuming you're talking about homework for the afternoon class, you've never been too fond of the other kind of homework."

They smiled back cheekily and Jamie asked, "Can she stay for lunch?"

"If she asks her mum first, she can!" Constance said.

When they reached the kitchen, Cali called her mum on the Peekaboo and they sat down to a lively lunch. After lunch they went back upstairs to practice some more. By the time Cali left; the boys had perfected the spell and they had made plans to meet in the morning to go to the entrance of the valley.

* * * *

Sunday morning dawned clear and bright, Nicky and Jamie awoke early with the anticipation of an adventure ahead. They washed and dressed and were whispering excitedly as they left Nicky's room, when a voice behind them said,

"And what are you two up to huh?" They jumped and spun around to look straight into the smiling green eyes of their mother who had just come out of her room.

"Nothing, we didn't want to wake you up" Jamie said thinking quickly

"Sure you didn't and I guess that it's just a coincidence that you're already washed and dressed and it's not even eight o'clock yet." she replied, smiling even more.

They all walked down to the kitchen together. Constance stoked up the fire in the stove while Jamie filled the kettle and Nicky brought out the eggs, bacon and bread from the pantry. While Constance cooked the breakfast and the boys set the table she asked,

"What are you two really doing up so early, are you meeting up with that nice girl? What's her name? Cali?"

"Yeah, Caliandra Pendoggett, she's going to take us exploring this morning", Nicky said, not looking at his mother.

"I know her mother, we used to go to school together and I'm sure I don't have to remind you to stay inside the valley, do I?" she looked at the boys who were trying to look busy, "It could be dangerous if you go out, you know that, right?"

"Yes mum!" the boys said innocently.

Just as they were finishing their breakfast, there was a knock at the kitchen door, Nicky got up to answer it, Cali was standing there smiling, she saw Constance standing behind Nicky and said, "Good morning Mrs. Elder!"

"Good morning Cali, how's your mother?"

"She's fine, she says to say hello and would like you to go and have tea one morning" answered Cali.

"That's very nice of her, tell her I'd be happy to".

By this time the boys had put on their coats and were waiting for Cali at the door. They said goodbye and left.

"Did you bring the dust?" asked Cali when they were away from the kitchen door.

"Yeah, it's in my pocket" replied Jamie, tapping his leg.

The wind rustling through the trees and the birds singing were the only sounds they could hear as they strolled down towards the village; it was a normal quiet Sunday morning as they walked past the village green; all the shops were closed and no one was about. They passed the last couple cottages and quickened their pace along the dirt road. The last time the boys had been here was when they arrived, it seemed a lot different now, they remembered the branches of the trees scraping the side of the station-wagon, they now new why, the further they went the narrower the road got until it was no more than a dirt track with tall trees on either side; their thick canopy meeting overhead and blocking out the daylight.

Up ahead they could barely see the entrance, but Cali stepped to the side of the road and the boys followed.

"The entrance is just ahead so we'd better do it here" ,she whispered. Jamie reached into his pocket and pulled out the bag of dust, in turn they all took a handful, recited the spell and vanished.

"Okay, lets go!", Jamie whispered, but the only problem was, they couldn't see each other, they could only hear their footsteps on the dirt road. Jamie walked into Cali who, in turn, stepped on the back of Nicky's heel, which made his shoe come off and then Jamie fell over Nicky, who had stopped to put his shoe back on, then Cali walked into Jamie. Soon they were laughing so hard that they couldn't walk. When they had calmed down, Cali suggested they link arms and they continued on down the road.

At the entrance, they saw two black cars across the road with four warlocks standing next to them, talking quietly together. Seconds later, two of them got into one of the cars and left.

Jamie said, "Must be a shift change".

Cali whispered, "Now remember, you two cannot get back into the valley without me, so we have to stay close together, the spells won't work through the veil, so we have to go out".

They hung onto each other and crept out to the crossroads. Jamie took out the other bag of dust from his pocket as they snuck up to the side of the car. They could hear the two warlocks complaining on the other side of the car. Jamie took a handful of dust and passed the bag to Nicky, who also took a handful and together they said, "Stupefacere" and blew the dust into the faces of the warlocks. The warlocks stopped talking and stood motionless against the car.

Cali said "Vail of Light, Shroud of might, Bring me back to sight."

She reappeared and walked up to one of the warlocks and made faces at him, but he just stood there with a blank expression on his face. One at a time, she took them by the hand and led them over to a tree and said, "Sit!", they sat, she said, "Close your eyes!" and they closed their eyes. She walked back to Nicky and Jamie, who had also re-appeared, and said,

"We should see how long it lasts, let's get back under the veil, just in case they come out of it suddenly".

So the three of them walked back across the road and waited, just beyond the entrance. Cali started timing them, fifteen minutes, half an hour, three quarters, an hour. The boys had become bored and started wrestling.

Cali snapped, "This is serious, we need to know how long this lasts it could mean the difference between life and death, YOURS!"

The boys stopped wrestling and sat up.

Nicky said "How long has it been now?"

"One hour and ten minutes." Cali answered.

At that moment, they noticed one of the warlocks was moving; he rubbed his eyes and staggered up from the ground. He tried to wake the other one but he wasn't moving. The warlock staggered around the car, looking for anything suspicious, but saw nothing (he couldn't see the entrance to the valley). Soon his companion started to move and stagger to his feet. They started a heated argument about what had happened, the kids decided that this would be a good time to suddenly appear and hopefully trick them into trying a black spell, so they could practice the Counter-spell spell.

Instantly, seemingly out of nowhere, three kids popped up on the road. The warlocks were startled and one yelled, "Crucificare, Crucify!" and sparks shot from his hand. Micro-seconds later, the boys yelled "Contra Spellam" and threw out their hands, the sparks hit their hands and dissipated, but at the same time the other warlock yelled "Hurtare Brutus" at the boys, but Cali jumped in front and yelled "Contra Spellam" and, without waiting to see the results, she grabbed the boys by the arms and dragged them back into the valley with the warlocks in hot pursuit. They didn't stop running until they were half way towards the village.

Cali turned her head to make sure they hadn't got in and then came to a stop, with her hands on her knees, breathing very hard. The boys also stopped and collapsed on the grass verge, laughing with excitement and fear.

"That was awesome; did you see the look on his face when it didn't work?" Jamie said panting.

"Yeah and the other one when he yelled, I thought he was going to get us!" Nicky said, giggling nervously.

Only Cali was calm, she said, "We survived, barely, if I hadn't been there, that second one would have hit you and it would have been over, you two have to work out a system, you can't both do a Counter-spell for one spell".

The boys stopped laughing and looked at her, she was right. They had screwed up and they were lucky to have got away with it. And now they couldn't go back again because the warlocks would probably be expecting them.

She said more kindly, "We don't know if the Counter-spell from both of you worked or just one and if just one, which one? We're going to have to find someone who will be willing to use a spell against you."

"Charlotte will probably do it" Nicky said.

"Okay then we'll go and ask her," said Jamie.

The three of them got up and sauntered off through the village reliving the adventure, this time Cali joined in. Back at the Mansion, they found Charlotte sitting by the kitchen door,

Nicky walked over, bent down, and whispered, "Do you want in?"

"I've been waiting for you, I'll meet you in the summerhouse" and she trotted off.

The kids looked at each other, wondering what was wrong. They followed her to the summerhouse, where they found her waiting by the broken window. Jamie opened it and they all climbed in. But Charlotte didn't transform.

"What's wrong, why don't you change?" Nicky asked.

"I'm having difficulty changing back and forth, so I'm doing as little of it as possible, but that's not why I was waiting for you, where did you go this morning?" she asked sternly.

"We tried out those spells you taught us, on the warlocks at the entrance, it was great!" Jamie said, smiling proudly.

"Yeah we beat 'em, we did the Stupefy Spell first and then when they came out of it, we got them to do black magic and we did the Counter-spell spell", Nicky said excitedly.

"What were you thinking? That was very dangerous, you could've been caught!" Charlotte said angrily.

"We were only doing what you taught us" Jamie said, feeling hurt.

"I didn't teach you to be reckless!", Charlotte yelled.

Cali piped up, "You wanted them to learn, they were trying the spells against each other, there was no way of knowing if they were working or not, I suggested the warlocks, I was with them and I have been doing spells since I was four and I'm the top of my class", she said hoping not to sound too boastful. "But it didn't go exactly as planned, they both used the Counter-spell Spell together, so we still don't know if both of them can do it or not. They want to ask you something." she finished, sounding quite deflated.

"Err.. yeah.. we need you to try a spell on us individually so we can see if we can do the Counter-spell Spell." Nicky said quietly.

"Why didn't you ask me first, oh never mind, you weren't hurt and you proved you can do the Stupefying Spell, how long did it last, did you time it?" Charlotte asked.

"Almost an hour and quarter!" Cali said proudly.

"Good, good, that should give you enough time. Tonight, after everyone's gone to bed, come down to the cellar and we'll practice for an hour. I've got to go now" and she jumped nimbly through the window and was gone.

"Do you think she's okay? What's this about having difficulty changing?" Nicky asked.

"The people who have the ability to transform into animals" Cali explained, "sometimes, when they get old, they lose the ability to transform; if they're not careful they get stuck as the animal and in time, lose the ability to talk but gain telepathic ability. In other words, they become the animal but with a mixture of animal and human brains. That's how the story of familiars came about, they weren't just normal animals, they were witches or wizards who couldn't change back, but were still capable of doing simple spells and they became helpers to the Specials."

* * * *

As the grandfather clock in the entrance hall struck eleven, the boys silently closed the library door and descended into the cellar. Charlotte was waiting for them; she had transformed and was sitting in the armchair beside the fire. She looked over as they entered, smiled and looked back at the fire. The boys walked over and Nicky sat in the other armchair.

He said "Are you feeling alright? You're not sick or anything are you?"

"No dear, I'm just old and I'm finding it harder to do what I used to do", she said softly.

"You don't have to spend so much time helping us, if that would make a difference" Jamie said with concern.

"That's sweet Jamie, but I enjoy helping you two, I feel useful again, if I didn't have to transform so much to go outside that would help, and my eyesight's not what it used to be!" she said, smiling.

"We can bring you dinner every night if you want?" Nicky said still concerned.

"Well maybe not every night, your aunt might notice food disappearing", she replied, "but we had better get down to business or you won't be able to get up tomorrow morning."

They moved to a clear area in the chamber and started to practice. Charlotte told Jamie to go first, she tried a giggle spell, but Jamie wasn't quick enough and ended up giggling for about ten minutes, which, of course, is very contagious, so they all ended up helplessly giggling! Charlotte decided that maybe the giggle spell wasn't the best one to use, so she tried a wart spell. Jamie, not wanting to end up with warts all over his body, concentrated much harder. This time he succeeded in blocking it.

Next she tried a hair-growing spell on Nicky and he managed to block almost all of it but he did get a tuft of hair growing out of his ear. Charlotte fixed this with a reverse spell and tried again, this time he grew a tuft of hair on his chin. Nicky practiced for almost an hour and, finally, could master the spell perfectly.

Nicky sat down in the armchair while Charlotte tried with Jamie, even though he had got it right, she needed to make sure he could do it every time. They practiced for maybe another half an hour until Charlotte said that she was feeling quite exhausted and needed to go to bed. The boys gave her a hug, promised to bring her some food in the morning so she didn't have to go hunting and left.

Lying in his bed later, Nicky thought about the spells they had gone up against. He, absentmindedly, rubbed his chin, which was now hair free, thought how hard he had found it. The

Stupefying Spell was easy and so was the Invisibility one but the Counter-spell..... well, he wasn't sure he liked the idea of having to go up against someone who might want to seriously hurt or worse still, kill him.

Chapter Thirteen

Agatha's Diary

The Spring holidays were finally here and, because the boys had been working so hard practicing spells, they decided they were entitled to a day off and the first thing they were going to do was to explore the beach. Last time they had just played in the surf, but this time they wanted to explore some caves they had seen but couldn't get to as the tide was in.

So, right after breakfast they left the Mansion and headed for the beach. It was quite windy but the sun was shining and, unless they were in the shade, it was quite warm, but, of course, on the beach it was a different story; it was bitterly cold and the surf was breaking very high over the reef. The reef worked as a natural fortification, Jamie had read in "The History of the Padstows" that many a ship had been destroyed on it, but the fishermen from the valley had persevered and found a passage through to open sea where they would fish. This passage had been lost when the fishermen, like many others, didn't feel safe in the valley and had moved away after the Witchfinder had nearly destroyed the village. The only things left to remind anyone that there had ever been fishermen here were the steps down to the beach and a few piles of stones that were ones the walls of their cottages.

The beach was actually a cove with cliffs rising high on three sides. The cave the boys had seen was on the furthest point and, when the tide was in, the entrance flooded but today the tide was out and so they scrambled over the rocks to the entrance that really wasn't much more than a crevasse carved out of the cliffs by the sea over many centuries.

Jamie turned on his torch, as they entered. The cave smelled strongly of dead shellfish, underfoot the sand was still damp from the tide and was littered with pieces of seaweed. A crab scurried away as they entered. It was very dark and the torchlight made it look spooky. The ground rose slightly as they went deeper into the cliff and the walls closed in until they could touch both walls by simply holding out their arms. Soon, the ground began to rise quite steeply and the sand became dry under their feet. The boys, puffing slightly from the climb, scrambled through small openings and over boulders, until finally the ground levelled off and the trek was easier.

Suddenly, something small and black whipped past Jamie's head and a strange flapping noise nearly deafened them. Jamie flashed the torchlight around the walls and over the ceiling and there, hanging from the ceiling, were hundreds of bats, upside down and flapping their wings. The boys, with their hearts still rapidly pounding, gave a nervous laugh and moved further into the cave.

Deeper and deeper they went into the cliff. Nicky said, feeling unnerved by the bats, "How far does this go, maybe we should go back, in case the tide comes in?"

"The tide won't come in for awhile yet, don't you want to see where this leads?" Jamie asked, looking at Nicky.

"Yeah, of course I do, I was just worried about you getting trapped by the sea, you know, 'cos you can't swim, that's all" Nicky said, trying to sound casual.

"I don't think this can go much further, it looks like it narrows quite a bit up there" Jamie said, flashing the torch ahead of him.

The boys were now walking slightly crouched over as the cave had shrunk drastically, but still they kept going. They climbed over another boulder and came out into a larger cavern. Jamie straightened up and came to a stop in front of a wall of rock, his torch searching this way and that. Nicky moved beside Jamie and walked along the wall looking at the rock too. Then he was gone! Jamie couldn't believe his eyes, one minute he was looking at Nicky, about to say they had better turn back and the next, Nicky had vanished! Jamie yelled and Nicky's head popped out of the rocks smiling.

"What are you yelling at?"

"You vanished, one minute you were there and the next you were gone. Where's the rest of you?" Jamie said, a little panicky.

Nicky stepped back beside Jamie and said, "Come and look at this!"

Jamie moved over to where Nicky was standing and saw what Nicky had done. Looking straight at the rock wall it looked solid, but as he stepped to one side and stood very close to the wall there was a small gap, less than two feet wide, the right side was set back from the left, you had to be right up against the wall to see it.

The boys squeezed through the gap and entered a much larger cave. Jamie's torch flashed around the walls to reveal torches hanging from sconces and a solid wooden door on the furthest wall of the cave. Jamie dug in his pocket for a match and lit the torches. The cave was bathed in warm yellow light. They crossed to the door and lifted the big heavy ring and turned it, they pulled as hard as they could on the ring and, to their surprise, the door opened really easily and sent them flying backwards.

But at the same moment a low growl met their ears and before they had time to scramble to their feet and close the door, a huge, hairy, black head, with gnashing teeth and flashing black eyes appeared in the doorway. A massive leg with matted fur and enormous paws came out of the darkness, then another leg, followed by a shaggy body, and two more legs and a large bushy tail. The boys scrambled backwards on all fours, the animal towering over them, its fangs bared and a long string of drool dangling from its mouth. The black eyes were staring straight at them, unblinking! The boys lay on the floor too terrified to move. The beast now emerged from the darkness, revealing a tangled mass of fur and dirt over its shaggy black body, It was the size of a baby elephant, but resembled a baby Hairy Mammoth.

Jamie finally found his voice and nervously but soothingly, in a soft voice said "Hi boy, what a pretty boy, there's a nice doggy, please don't eat us," and to their surprise, the dog stopped growling, pricked up its ears, cocked its head to one side and, very slowly, his very long bushy tail began to wag. Feeling encouraged, Jamie said, as he held out his hand to the animal, "Yeah, nice boy, come to Jamie, yeah good boy!" And before he knew what was happening, the animal flopped down beside him and rolled over onto its back.

Jamie slowly started rubbing its belly and looked helplessly at Nicky; Nicky gingerly kneeled next to the animal and also began rubbing its belly. The drool began to flow from its mouth, soaking the ground where it landed. After a few minutes, the boys were able to stand up and the animal did too. They realised that it was just a big soppy thing, running around them, knocking their legs out from under them as it circled happily and its tail smacked them in the chest as it wagged.

The boys moved towards the door, but again the animal jumped in front of them and growled. Shocked, they stopped and stared at it. Why wouldn't it let them through the door? Jamie tried to peer around the animal but it was very dark and he couldn't see anything. Nicky found some biscuits in his pocket and tried to bribe the animal with them but he just took them and growled again. Jamie had an idea,

"How about taking it out onto the beach and playing with it for a while." He couldn't understand how an animal this big got into the cave in the first place let alone behind a closed door. "Maybe this is a pirates cave and they left the dog here to protect their treasure?"

"But why would they leave it locked in the room?" Nicky asked.

"Don't know, but I bet it would like some fresh air and the water."

The animal sort of reminded Nicky of a dog he had seen in a book once, called a Newfoundlander. A Newfoundlander was a working dog that would pull boats to shore when people got into difficulty at sea. If it wasn't for the fangs and the fact that it was twice the size of any dog he'd ever seen, it could be mistaken for one.

So the boys started to walk back along the cave calling "the dog" to follow. It whimpered as they moved away from it and looked as if it wanted to follow but kept looking back behind the door. As they moved out of sight, it gave a deafening, booming bark, then another whimper. The boys felt bad so they turned back and, as soon as it saw them, it started jumping around on the spot. They called it again, patted their knees and finally it came bounding over to them; they skipped out of its way just in time before it bowled them over.

It followed them along the cave, whimpering and stopping, until the boys called it again. This went on again and again until they finally made it back to the beach. The dog reached the entrance but again stopped and whimpered, but this time it was trembling too as it stared at the waves pounding the rocks. The boys thought it was acting as if it had never seen waves before, but how could it get in the cave if it hadn't gone in from the beach.

The boys patiently and calmly coaxed the dog to come out and finally; it walked over to them where it nervously tried to lick their faces. It took a few more encouragements to get the dog to play and soon they were running along the beach with it jumping up at them and having a great time. Before they knew what was happening, it ran into the sea and was trying to catch the waves in its very large mouth; the boys stood there laughing until the dog ran back towards them and then, shook the water out of its coat and soaked the boys from head to toe.

After, what seemed to be ages, the boys fell to the sand exhausted from running up and down the beach with the dog. The dog came over and licked both their faces with one very large, soaking-wet tongue and then laid down beside them panting, his hot breath warming their cold ears. Jamie said thoughtfully,

"What are we going to do with him now, we can't take him to the Mansion, can we?"

"It doesn't seem fair to take him back to the cave, look how happy he is with us." Nicky said, scratching behind one enormous floppy ear.

But they didn't have to make the decision because the dog suddenly jumped up and stared at the sea, and the boys saw what it saw, the tide was coming in and, before they could say or do anything, the dog ran off along the beach to the cave and disappeared inside. The boys ran after it but it was much faster than they were and by the time they reached the rocks, the tide was already covering them and they knew that if they followed it inside the cave, they would be trapped. The only thing they could hope for was that the dog made it back to the big cave and didn't get trapped.

The boys stayed on the beach watching the entrance to the cave until the tide was completely in, just in case the dog came out again and when they were sure that the sea had blocked its way, they walked slowly towards the steps back up to the Mansion.

"We're coming back to see it again, aren't we?" Nicky asked, looking at Jamie as they crossed the lawn.

"Yeah, we'll come back tomorrow and we'll bring some food with us, I don't know what it's been eating and I'm not sure I want to, but I'm sure it will like Auntie's cooking." Jamie said smiling.

The following morning, with a bag of leftovers, the boys headed down to the beach, they retraced their steps through the cave until they arrived in front of the door, they called out to the dog and they heard the deep growl.

"It's okay boy its just us, come and see what we have for you." Jamie said softly, and as they stood back, the dog appeared in the doorway, baring its teeth and still growling. It took a few seconds before the dog seemed to recognise them and then cautiously he came to them, they opened the bag of food and the dog devoured every bit.

After that, the dog was bounding around them enjoying the scratching and petting. As they had yesterday, the boys tried to get to the door and again the dog jumped in front of them and growled, so the boys played with him some more and tried again. They repeated this again and again until, after about an hour, the dog finally let them in.

The boys weren't really prepared for what they saw. Covering the floor were the bones of small animals and rodents mixed with the dog droppings and it smelled foul. Water was running down from an underground stream over on one side next to a clean area, which was obviously the dog's sleeping area and a small hole, way above them, let in a dim light.

On the far side was another door that the boys were now picking their way to, the dog following closely behind, until he realised where they were going and he ran in front of them, blocking their way.

"Oh, come on boy, we're not going through that again are we? Come here boy' Jamie said, patting his knees.

The dog took a step forward but stopped. Both boys patted their knees and called him, this time, with tail between his legs, he walked over to them and gave Jamie the chance to open the door. Jamie stepped inside and screamed with fright as the light from his torch fell across a small bed, Nicky jumped and the dog growled and ran passed Jamie into the room and laid down beside the small bed, where a skeleton lay under a blanket.

The boys stood frozen to the spot, with all kinds of thoughts going through their heads. Nicky was the first one to take his eyes off the bed and look towards a small table off to one side. He walked over to it and lit the oil lamp sitting there. He picked it up, turned towards the bed and slowly walked over to it with Jamie beside him. The dog gave a little whimper, looked at the skeleton, and then put its head down on its paws with a sad look on his face. Nicky bent down and stroked the dog's head and its tail gently swept the floor.

Jamie was trying to inspect the skeleton without disturbing it; he didn't think the dog would be too happy if he actually touched it. He noticed that it was wearing a very old fashioned dress with a disintegrating lace collar and around its neck; a gold chain was just visible. He reached down and gently pulled the chain out; attached to it was a small locket which, when he opened it, found himself looking into the faces of Charlotte's mother, Margaret, and her aunt Emily. He also noticed that a ring, loosely around one finger, was the same as his aunt's. There were some strands of reddish blonde hair lying on the pillow. Jamie was quite convinced that they had found the remains of Agatha.

Nicky straightened up and crossed over to the table. He picked up a very dusty book, wiped the dust off with his sleeve and opened it up. On the first page he read, aloud;

"To anyone who might find this, this is the story of Agatha Ballystock.

After my sister Margaret died and that idiot of a husband of hers would not let me bring her back, I was locked in the tower, he said I was crazy and should be locked away in an asylum. I was in the tower for almost two years before he decided he was going to poison me, or maybe it was that housekeeper of his, she seems to have too much influence over him.

I realised that they were trying to slowly poison me when I became ill after every meal, so I decided that I must escape. The spell I had been working on to turn into an animal and at the same time dematerialise outside the Mansion was not going to work; it was too dangerous to try, so I abandoned it. I decided on a simpler plan, if I could use a spell to reduce my pulse and heartbeat so it wasn't detectible, I could fool them into thinking I was dead and when they took me out of the tower, I would then escape.

Little did I realise that he was so unscrupulous as to try and bury me on the estate instead of calling the undertaker and having me buried in the graveyard. But when he left me in the stables to go and dig my grave, I awoke and made my escape. I think from this point on, it pushed him over the edge because I used to see him sitting in the dining room late at night, drinking until he passed out and then that housekeeper would have to get the groom to put him to bed, until the groom quit and she just left him there.

My only regret is that I could not save Charlotte from the same fate as they had planned for me. By the time I realised she was locked in the tower, he had already killed her and from that point on I swore he was not going to profit from his evil doings. I became his night stalker, he thought I was a ghost and would be terrified, and I would tell him that he would pay for his evil doings and, in time, he drank himself to death. It was a bad end to a bad man.

I lived in this cave with only Oscar (a Manta, but not just an ordinary Manta, he had been bewitched by someone and was very intelligent and could come out of the water when the tide went out), and a puppy that had fallen through the hole in the outer cave. When I realised that I was dying from the poison, I decided I would put my essence into the puppy but I would need to use a magical creature to transfer my essence.

So when Oscar (who turned out to be female) had babies I used a spell to combine the puppy, the baby Manta and my essence, but what I didn't count on was the puppy being the dominant ingredient, so instead of the Manta growing and living hundreds of years with my essence, the puppy grew huge and had only the Manta's life span and very little of my essence. So while I wither away in this cave, the puppy has grown and has become my guardian.

Now at the end of my life, and I know I only have days left, I don't have the strength to take the dog out of the cave and even if I did I don't think he would stay away. If I lock him out of my room he just whines and scratches at the door until I let him in. I am hoping that when I have gone, he will find his way out of the cave and to a new home.

I think I will take a nap now, I'm feeling very tired, I've put him in the other room hoping he will go for a walk outside, but I can hear him whining at the door, I'll try and finish later."

The boys looked at each other and both said at the same time, "So who's been feeding the dog all these years?"

"I have" said a voice from behind them and the boys were so startled that they nearly collided as they spun around. Standing in the doorway was the tabby cat.

"How did you know he was down here and why didn't you take him out?" asked Nicky.

"I first heard him howling years and years ago, when I was hunting. I followed the sound and found the hole, but couldn't get down it so I used to throw the food down to him. I kept searching for the entrance, then after a while I found the cave, but I kept coming to a dead end. So I continued to feed him through the hole, and then today I heard you two talking down here so I came to see how you had managed to find the dog and as I've been having difficulty changing, I stayed transformed and followed your scent, leading me right to you".

"Yeah, we found the dog yesterday" said Jamie "and made friends with him and today he let us in here, I think you should read this!" and he held out Agatha's diary.

"I heard everything," Charlotte said softly, crossing the room to look at the skeleton. "Will you take the locket for me Jamie?"

Jamie looked at the dog with scepticism. "I think he understands." Charlotte said.

The dog whimpered as if he understood that Jamie wasn't going to do any harm and gently nudged his elbow with his wet nose as if to say take it.

Charlotte looked down into the black eyes and quietly said, "So you do have some of Aunt Agatha's essence in you, we will give her a proper burial, won't we boys? And then you can come and live with me or the boys if you would prefer".

And again as if he understood, he stood up and licked her face and then walked over and laid down beside Nicky.

* * * *

Back at the Mansion the boys said goodbye to Charlotte and walked to the kitchen, where they found their mum and aunts.

"You'll never guess what we found in a cave, mum?" said Nicky, his eyes sparkling.

"What, dear?" answered Constance, without looking up from her potions book.

"We found Agatha Ballystock!" chirped in Jamie.

"Who, dear?" said Constance, still not paying any attention.

"Agatha Ballystock!" Nicky repeated, somewhat disappointed at not getting the reaction he'd expected.

"You mean Agatha that disappeared years and years ago?" said Lydia, turning to see their excited faces.

"Yeah, we found her skeleton in a cave on the beach." said Jamie smiling.

"And a great big dog. Well, I think it's a dog!" said Nicky.

"Hang on a minute, you're telling us that you two have just solved one of the biggest mysteries of this valley, in just a few months, a mystery that no-one has been able to solve in a hundred years?" said Amy, flabbergasted.

"Yeah, I guess that's what we're saying," said Jamie, puffing out his chest.

"I don't believe it, show me!" said Amy.

"Are you two playing some kind of a trick on us?" said Constance, suspiciously.

"No honest, mum, we really have found her and she left a diary to say what happened to her. Come on, we'll show you!" Nicky said, moving to the door.

After some convincing, Constance and Amy followed the boys to the cave to see for themselves. When they returned to the Mansion, with Agatha's diary, Lydia asked

"So was it a hoax?"

Without saying anything Amy handed the diary to Lydia. She gently opened it and read. She looked up, a look of awe across her face.

"You actually found Agatha.... oh my word.... we must do something,....call someone, what should we do? She asked flustered, looking from one sister to the other.

"I think the first thing we should do is get Morton and couple of the other men to retrieve her remains, but first I think the boys are going to have to bring the "dog" to the mansion for a bath" said Constance. "I'm not sure he will let anyone near the remains without the boys being their, we had quite the time with him didn't we Amy?"

"I really thought he was going to eat one of us, but the boys seem to have a way with him and convinced him to let us in" answered Amy.

"We will have to let Teddy be there when they take Agatha out so he can see she's not there anymore or he will keep going back" Nicky said.

"Teddy?" said Constance

"Yeah he reminds me of a big... very big Teddy Bear" Nicky answered.

"Yeah that's a great name, Teddy Bear" Jamie said approvingly.

And the boys set about convincing their mum that the dog wouldn't be any trouble. They were allowed to keep him on the condition that they bath him regularly, cut out all the matted fur and have him sleep in the stable not in their rooms.

Lydia set about making arrangements to have Agatha's remains recovered while Amy made arrangements for a proper burial service. The following Sunday, the whole village turned out to say a long overdue goodbye to Agatha, the tabby cat and the big dog were right there beside Jamie and Nicky, and, except for Cali, only the boys knew what it meant to Charlotte to see her aunt buried properly.

Chapter Fourteen

The Rescue

On Wednesday, Jamie, Nicky and Cali spent most of the day in the summerhouse, practising spells, with a very large dog running around outside chasing anything and everything that moved. Cali had been very curious and a little upset that she hadn't been involved in their latest adventure, but with the promise that they wouldn't leave her out again, they got down to practicing some of the spells from a new spell book Cali had brought with her.

They had gone through it trying to find spells they could use against warlocks. They practiced the Silent Spell; this robbed the hapless receiver of the ability to talk, which the kids decided was good because they wouldn't be able to do a reversing spell or raise the alarm. They also practiced the Binding Spell, which bound the hands and feet together with an unbreakable invisible cord. They had also found some potions that looked promising, if they could get the ingredients. Cali said she would check her mum's supplies and the boys promised to ask Charlotte, as well as check out the house.

By late afternoon they were very confident that they were ready to make a plan for the rescue of their father. Cali said she would be back the following morning to help with the planning.

At supper that night, Cali and her parents were sitting around the table in the spotlessly clean kitchen of their home. Cali's father was a short stocky man with a shock of black hair, big bushy moustaches and black eyes, which, right now, were flashing angrily.

"The Council's very concerned for the safety of Roger Elder, it seems Ostrogoth is getting impatient and is threatening to send him back in little pieces." He stuffed another mouthful of food in his mouth, "The Council can't make a decision, I've told them it should be the Mansions' decision, they are the rightful owners of the Crystals and if they want to give the Crystal up, they should be allowed to!"

Cali's mother replied soothingly, "Don't get upset dear, you've told them what you think, it's up to them to make the decision. What about Milton Blueblood? Have you heard anymore from him?"

"He's gone missing, we don't know if he's been caught or just gone into hiding, we daren't send anyone else up there, we don't want to spook Ostrogoth into going who- knows-where." He threw down his knife and fork and sat back in his chair with a very disgruntled look on his face.

Cali's mother rose from the table, glided over to her husband and, with her very long, thin fingers began massaging his shoulders. He sighed and relaxed.

"I just feel so bad for them, they must be going crazy not being able to do anything. I know if you were taken my love, I would be trying everything in my power to get you back!" he said patting her hand.

"I know you would dear, and that's why I love you so much." She bent over and kissed him gently on the cheek.

Cali, her mind racing, excused herself. She ran up to her bedroom, grabbing up the Peekaboo from the hall table as she went by. Closing her door behind her, she sat on her bed and called for Nicky, but no one answered. She got up, walked to the window, and looked out. Should she walk over to the Mansion now? What excuse would she give for turning up unannounced? No, better try calling Nicky again, but again, no answer. There was a soft tab on her door, causing her to jump as if someone had pounded on the door.

"Come in!" she said.

"Did you take the... yes you did, haven't I told you a hundred times not to take the Peekaboo from the hall table, Cali?"

"Yes, sorry mum, I was trying to call the Mansion but no-ones answering."

"I expect they're in the living room and forgot to take it with them, was it important?" Cali's mum asked.

"No, not really, I just wanted to know what time we were getting together tomorrow," Cali said, hoping she sounded casual, "I'll just walk over in the morning".

* * * *

The next morning, bright and early, Cali was knocking on the Mansion's kitchen door, which was quickly answered by Nicky. Cali beckoned the boys outside just as Teddy Bear came charging over from the stables, where he had been sent to sleep after the aunts had seen how big he was.

"What's wrong?" Nicky said, trying to avoid being knocked over by the dog as it ran circles around them.

She beckoned again for them to follow and they crossed the courtyard to the stables . Slipping inside the ramshackle building, she said

"I tried to get hold of you last night to tell you what my dad was saying about Milton Blueblood being missing and that Ostrogoth is threatening to kill your dad. We have to attempt a rescue now!" she said frantically, ignoring the fact that Teddy Bear was jumping up at her. The boys both stared at her in disbelief.

"What do you mean we?" asked Nicky

"You promised you wouldn't leave me out of the next adventure" Cali said suspiciously.

"No, but we weren't talking about the rescue, it's too dangerous!" Jamie replied,

"Oh, so you think you'd have better luck without me, do you?" she asked, her dark eyes flashing with anger, very much like her father's had the previous evening.

"No, that's not what I meant!" Jamie said confused.

"I guess we had better start making a plan then." said Cali, putting an end to anymore argument

Jamie shook his head slightly and resigned himself to the fact that she was coming along and said

"So, first we have to get hold of a pocket globe."

"No, that's not direct enough, we don't know exactly where the island is, we're going to have to use the Travel Spell." Cali said.

"We don't know how to do that, wouldn't it be easier just to find out where Milton Blueblood was sending his reports from." Jamie said logically.

"And how do you expect me to ask my dad that?" asked Cali, getting slightly annoyed. "Oh by the way, dad, where is Milton Blueblood sending his reports from?" She said sarcastically reaching into her pocket and taking out something that looked like a pen. "I know how to do the spell and all you two have to do is hang onto the broomstick!"

"Broomstick? You're kidding right? A broomstick, that's so corny!" Jamie said laughing.

But Nicky was more interested in what Cali had taken out of her pocket; she tapped it twice on the wall and said, "Broomstick now!"

The "pen" levitated out of Cali's hand and transformed into a broomstick.

Jamie stopped laughing and stared at it, "Is that a real flying broomstick, can I ride it?"

"No, you don't ride it, you hold onto it, you think of where you want to go and say "Peregrinari". Shall we try?"

The boys nodded eagerly and held onto the broomstick. "Now think of the beach at the bottom of the cliff, then say it".

All three of them said, "Peregrinari" and, with a greenish-blue flash like a camera flash, they disappeared. A second later, another flash, this time on the beach at the bottom of the cliffs and all three re-appeared there. Nicky swayed a little upon landing and his head felt a little strange but apart from that, he was fine. They repeated it back into the stables.

"That was awesome, where can I get one?" Jamie asked excitedly.

Cali tapped it twice on the ground and it instantly became the size of a pen again, which she returned to her pocket, saying impatiently,

"You have to send away for them and they're not particularly cheap, now, can we get down to work?"

So they sat down on the hay bales and started planning the escape. As they planned, the tabby cat sauntered in through the crack in the door.

"What are you doing?" she asked.

"We have to rescue Dad now." Nicky said and went on to explain what Cali's dad had said.

"Are you prepared, have you learnt enough to protect yourselves?" she asked.

"We have some potions we would like to make, with your help." Nicky answered

"Which ones?"

"These!" Cali said opening the book and laying it on the ground so she could read them.

"We can do this one, and maybe this one, but that has to boil for a week. Collect up the ingredients, I have bat wings, hemlock and elf dust. If you can find the rest we can make them now in my place"

"Okay, lets get going, we don't have much time!" said Jamie.

They all nodded, stood up and left the stables, leaving Teddy Bear standing staring after them with his head cocked to one side and his ears raised as if he knew something was up.

The boys and Cali went off to search the kitchen pantry for the rest of the ingredients. It didn't take them long to find Lydia's stash. Charlotte disappeared around the corner of the Mansion and was soon entering the cellar by way of a small airshaft. She reached her kitchen and transformed, it took her a little longer than usual and she felt quite exhausted, but she had no time to rest. She shuffled over to the cupboard and picked the ingredients she needed, then shuffled back to the big wooden table and waited for the others

She didn't have long to wait; they came running down the steps, through the outer chamber and into hers.

"Hang the cauldron on the hook over the fire, please Jamie. Nicky start measuring out these and Cali chop up these." Charlotte said, handing jars and packets to Nicky and Cali. Soon the thin purple liquid was bubbling in the cauldron. "Have you memorised the spell to go with this?" Charlotte asked.

The boys looked at each other and said, "What spell?"

"The spell to banish them for all time." she answered.

"Err.... does that mean what I think it means?" Nicky asked.

"Sometimes you have to fight evil with a little evil of your own. They will be sent into oblivion!" Charlotte replied.

"I don't know if I can do that." Nicky said, with a shaky voice.

"Would you be able to if a warlock was about to put a death curse on your brother?" asked Cali. "Think of it as sending them back to hell, which is where most of them came from anyway." said Charlotte callously.

"What happens if you don't say the spell but just use the potion?" Nicky asked.

"There's no telling where they would go, they could be sent to hell or just part way, either way they won't be coming back to hurt anyone again." said Charlotte.

Nicky didn't answer, he was sure he would do anything to protect his brother, but sending someone to hell, he wasn't sure he was capable of that and really hoped he wouldn't have to find out. He was lost in his own thoughts and caught only the end of a conversation the others were having.

"I'll be coming with you and this isn't up for discussion, you may need more powerful magic than you can manage, but I'll have to come as a cat, my old body is too fragile. When had you planned to leave?"

"We were thinking about midnight tonight. That way our parents won't miss us until morning and by then we will be back, with Dad" Jamie said confidently.

"We'll meet in the stables at midnight then." Said Charlotte.

* * * *

The fire in Jamie's room was just embers as he silently got dressed. Nicky opened the door between their rooms, he was dressed in jeans and t-shirt with a sweatshirt over his arm and he was carrying his shoes. They didn't speak. Jamie picked up the two drawstring bags, tossed one to Nicky, and put the other in his pocket. He picked up his shoes and they tiptoed over to the door. Two minutes later, they pulled open the old creaky door of the stables and, a few seconds later; the cat came through the gap with a small bag around her neck.

"Take the bag please Jamie and hand one of the bottles to Nicky, you keep one and when Cali gets here, give her one too." she said.

Jamie pulled the bag over Charlotte's head and opened it. Inside were three vials of dark purple liquid. He handed one to Nicky and put one in his pocket. They stood nervously waiting for Cali. There was a flash of greenish-blue light and she stood in front of them. Jamie handed her a vial and she too put it in her pocket.

Charlotte said, "Let's get going!"

The trio tiptoed up the service road, following behind the cat, the wind was very cold and their teeth started to chatter. Charlotte led the kids through the village; all the cottages were dark, the only light came from the full moon. At the edge of the village green, past the last cottage, she led them into the trees. Jamie turned on his torch as the trees blocked the moon's light. They followed her along a narrow path deep into the woods; they were heading towards the road, but at an angle away from the entrance.

Cali stopped. "Why are we going this way, the entrance is over there?" she said, pointing to the left.

"I know but we don't want to go to the entrance, we don't need to encounter warlocks before we have to." Charlotte answered and Cali fell quiet and continued walking. The woods grew darker as the trees became thicker and the path wended its way through the trees. Charlotte stopped beside a large oak tree at the end of the path; the kids stopped and looked around; the path went nowhere, there was just a small hill in front of them.

Charlotte called Cali over and said, "I want you to touch that knot on the tree with your right hand and that knot with your left and then kiss the bark between the two."

Cali looked at her as if she was nuts. "Please!" Charlotte added. So Cali did what she was asked and, to their surprise, a small wooden door appeared in the hill. Jamie leant forward and opened it. Charlotte stepped through and the kids followed her into a dark narrow low tunnel.

As the ground sloped downwards the ceiling grew higher; tree roots hung down from the ceiling like tentacles, brushing the tops of their heads and making them shiver. With only Jamie's torch to guide them, they followed the tunnel for about ten minutes until the ground started to slope upwards again. At the end of the tunnel was another small wooden door, which Charlotte asked Jamie to open. She led them into a musky room with a dirt floor and thick stonewalls. A flight of wooden stairs against the far wall was the only thing in the room. Cali was the last to step into the room and as she did so, the door vanished.

"That's okay, it's a protection spell so that no-one can get into the valley without knowing where the door is, and once we go past the centre of the room, we will be outside the Vail of Protection. Ready? Okay, let's go!" and she led them up the rickety wooden stairs and into the hallway of an old cottage.

"Whose house is this?" Nicky asked.

"It's the village's, we use it if we have to deal with Normals, that way we don't have to take them into the valley, they can come to the house and it looks like whatever the visitor thinks the Specials home would look like".

"What do you mean?" Jamie asked.

"Well.... say your Aunt Amy needed to meet with a Normal. She would invite them in and they would see a home hung with macramé and bead curtains or, if your mum was meeting someone here they would see a smart modern home."

"That's neat, but why do they need a house like that?" asked Nicky.

"Because sometimes it's necessary for us to deal with Normals, like your mum for instance, she had to meet the Normals' Police here to explain where she had been and why she hadn't contacted them, it was a little hard to explain, but with a little simple spell, they accepted the explanation"

"But how do you know if someone is coming to see you?" ask Jamie.

"Well that's another bit of magic! As you see, there's a phone here in the hall, when we have to deal with Normals, we give them a phone number, we all have one, it rings here and then it is relayed to whoever the call is for through their Peekaboo's, but of course, they don't see us, it works just like a Normals phone."

"That's pretty ingenious, who came up with that?" asked Nicky.

"Oh, it was a joint effort a long time ago," answered Charlotte, "Okay, let's get back to business, in the front room you go, that's right, there's more room in here."

The room was neatly arranged with a sofa and two matching armchairs, a couple of end tables with suitable knick-knacks on them, stood beside the chairs. A large mirror hung over the small fireplace and simple drapes framed the small-paned window.

"You will have to carry me, I don't want to transform," Charlotte said.

Nicky gently picked her up, Cali removed the broomstick from her pocket and said "Now we have to be perfectly clear what we are thinking about, we don't want to be torn in a dozen different directions. Think about the dock closest to the moving island, nothing else, got it?" The boys nodded nervously.

They all hung onto the broomstick and yelled, "Peregrinari!" There was a flash and they vanished. It was a rocky ride, not like the instant ride to the beach. Everything was spinning blue and green, every couple of seconds they could see a dock and they thought they were going to stop, but then it would start swirling again and the dock would fade away. Finally they saw a dock and the spinning began to slow down, the next second they were standing unsteadily on a dark, smelly dock. The only light was coming from the windows of a nearby pub, in the distance they could make out the faint outline of an island shrouded in mist.

"It's usually a lot smoother than that, but I guess with four minds at work it was bound to be bumpy," said Cali.

"Look!" Nicky said pointing. He had noticed a small powerboat coming out of the mist from the direction of the island. They quickly hid behind some crates littering the dock. The boat pulled into the dock and cut its engine. A warlock clambered out and headed to the pub a few hundred yards away.

Charlotte said quietly, "That's one of his followers! Do the Invisibility Spell and get into the boat, I doubt he's going to be in there for too long".

The kids held hands, so as not to bump into each other once they were invisible, cast the spell and vanished. One by one they stepped down into the boat and hid at the back behind the seats. Charlotte jumped in and hid under the seat. They waited and waited, fifteen minutes went by and they still waited; twenty minutes, they were getting cramped and uncomfortable; but just as they were about to get out and walk around, the pub door opened and the warlock came out, carrying a fairly large wooden box. He climbed into the boat and placed the box on the seat, started the engine and soon they were gliding over the water towards the island.

The boat disappeared into the mist and only the engine could be heard; the kids kept very quiet as they crouched behind the seat. Finally the boat slowed down and pulled into a cove, the warlock jumped out and pulled the boat up onto the beach. He picked up the box and headed towards a path leading inland.

When he was a safe distance away, the kids scrambled out of the boat and started to follow the warlock. It was a little difficult trying to walk in a single file when they couldn't see the person in front and they kept treading on the backs of each other's heels but this time they didn't laugh, they were much too tense to laugh. The cat led the way and, after a few minutes, stopped near the castle. They could see the warlock walking to a side door, which he pulled open; a beam of light lit up the pathway and they could hear talking coming from inside. He walked in and closed the door.

"Okay you three, we can't go in that way there's too many in that room, we have to find some way of getting in without anyone seeing a door open, but before we do that I want to do a little spell on you three so you can see each other. Hold still or I might miss, 'Visibili!'.... Is that better, can you see each other?"

"Yeah, we look like ghosts, I can see right through you, Jamie" Nicky said grinning.

"Can you see us, Charlotte?" Cali asked

"No, but I can sense where you are and that's just as good," she replied.

They turned and took a step but stopped suddenly.

"Where's the castle gone?" Nicky asked, astonished.

"Don't panic, they've just got an invisibility spell over it," said Charlotte.

"But how come we saw it a few minutes ago?" asked Jamie.

"Because the warlock knows the spell and obviously said it as he was walking towards the castle," replied Cali.

"How do we break it?" Nicky asked.

"I think a little chant should do it, don't you Cali, I don't think it's going to be a strong spell?" Charlotte said. Cali nodded.

"*Implementum, visibilis, Implementum visibilis, Implementum visibilis, Implementum visibilis*" Cali and Charlotte chanted together and, in seconds, the castle became visible. The group crept quietly along the track and began looking for a way in; they had circled almost the whole castle before Charlotte said, "Over here."

They quickly moved towards Charlotte and saw a small window barely above the ground. Jamie bent down and pulled it open, he beckoned Nicky to follow the cat inside but Nicky banged his head against something and fell backwards. Jamie put his hand out and touched what felt like a glass wall, but how could this be, Charlotte had got through. But as he patted over the opening of the window, it was obvious they couldn't get in, their way was blocked.

Charlotte called from inside the room, "What's taking you so long?"

"We can't get in, there's a force field or something!," Jamie said.

Charlotte jumped back through the window, with no problem. She thought for a moment and said, "I'll just have to try and transform you into animals, I haven't done this for awhile but it should be like riding a bike, you never forget...I hope!" she said with a twinkle in her eye, "Cali you go first".

Cali came forward and nervously stood in front of Charlotte.

"Animal, Manimal, creature inside, change this person to their spirit guide."

And suddenly Cali began to shrink, she got smaller and smaller, her nose became pointed and her nails began to grow, her front teeth began to protrude and black fur covered her sleek body. Fear gripped her and her instincts told her to run under the nearest bush.

"It's okay Cali, try and control your fear, you're a gerbil with all the gerbils instincts but remember you still have the ability to reason. That's right, good!" said Charlotte, as she noticed the panicky movements Cali was making calming down.

"You're next Nicky! 'Animal, manimal creature inside, change this person to their spirit guide' "

Nicky too, started to shrink and his arms began to spread out and grow feathers, his nose became hooked, his eyes turned yellow and beady, his feet turned to huge claws. He flapped his wings and soared into the sky before Charlotte had a chance to stop him. Cali's fears came flooding back as she watched the beautiful eagle soaring overhead and she scurried under the nearest bush for protection. Jamie held out his arm and Nicky landed gently on it.

Charlotte said, "Have you got control or are you going to eat your best friend?"

Nicky flew down to the ground and hopped over to Cali who was cowering under the bush, he said, in a squawky voice, "It's alright I'm not going to eat you."

"Thanks a lot, I wish I could get a grip on this fear, I never realised how scared gerbils were all the time!" Cali squeaked, coming out from under the bush.

"You ready Jamie?" asked Charlotte. And Jamie nodded; Charlotte repeated the spell for the third time.

Jamie also began to shrink, his nose started to twitch and a bushy tail sprouted from his backside, grey and white fur covered his body, he stood up on his hind legs looking around. He bounded over to Cali and Nicky and said, very fast, "This is great, I feel like looking for nuts!"

"Lets go kids, we're running out of time," said Charlotte, jumping back through the window.

One by one they jumped through the window, except Nicky of course; he flew through the window, they found themselves in a small room, full of supplies. Boxes of food were piled almost to the ceiling; there was just enough room for a person to squeeze between them to get to the door. The door was open a fraction and Charlotte, with her cat ears, listened for any sound coming from deeper inside the castle. It was all quiet, she pawed at the door until it was open enough for her to get through, and she looked around it and found it opened into a large, empty room.

The others followed Charlotte into the room and looked for an exit. There were two other doors, one lead to stairs going up to the floor above and the other to a long passageway, this was the one they decided to take. Nicky flew overhead while Cali and Jamie scampered along the dimly lit passageway and Charlotte ran along behind them. The first corner led to more rooms. At the second corner, a flight of stone steps led downwards, illuminated by torches burning in brackets on the wall. With the cat leading the way and the gerbil on the eagle's back, they followed the spiralling steps down. Jamie began to wonder why they hadn't encountered any real resistance yet, could Ostrogoth really be that confident that he felt he didn't need any guards on their father.

Just as he was about to say something to the cat, she suddenly stopped. They heard talking coming from further down the steps and it was getting closer. They quickly looked around for somewhere to hide. Nicky said, "Hang on!" and he flew down, grabbed Charlotte between his talons, soared to a ledge just below the ceiling, where he gently let her go, and landed beside her. Jamie scurried up the wall into the shadows and stayed very still. A few seconds later, two warlocks came up carrying a food tray.

One said, "I don' know why the Master don' just pu' 'im outta 'is misery, 'e's refusin' to ea' and e's not gonna be able to resist the truth spells much longer, I've never known a Normal to 'ave so much willpower, if I di'n' know be"a, I'd say someone pu' a protection spell on 'im." Their voices faded away and a few seconds later, Nicky picked up Charlotte and flew back down to the steps.

They continued down, the smell of seawater, mixed with rotting vegetation, became stronger and stronger as they descended. At the bottom, they came to a heavy wooden door, which was locked, but Cali could squeeze under it, so she volunteered to have a look around. She came back a few minutes later and squeaked,

"There's another door at the far end of the room, but I couldn't get to it because the floor is broken away. Those warlocks must know a way to fix it but I couldn't see a way, there's no switches or knobs or anything, it must be a spell."

"First things first, we have to get past this door before we can proceed!" Charlotte said, "Okay stand back! I'm going to try something".

"Not the same spell that destroyed half the tower?" Jamie said, looking worried.

"No dear, I've perfected another one over the years, who has the elf dust?"

"I do!" Nicky said, reaching under his breast feathers and pulling out the drawstring bag.

Charlotte said, "You have the best ability to hold things Jamie, take a pinch and hold it in front of the lock, Nicky flap your wings so it goes into the lock."

As Nicky flapped, Charlotte said, "Open door!" and the door flew open.

"That was simple!" Jamie said, impressed.

"The simple ones usually work the best, remember that Jamie!" Charlotte replied. "Now to get over to the other side of the room"

"I can help" Nicky said, "Cali climb on and Jamie stand still so I can pick you up"

Nicky picked up Jamie and flew to the other side of the room, dropped Jamie gently onto the ground and then landed so that Cali could climb off and then he flew back for Charlotte, picking her up gently and flying her to the other side.

The other door was unlocked, but being animals no one was big enough or strong enough to open it and Charlotte didn't have the strength to transform, so she performed a reversal spell on the kids. Jamie pulled open the heavy door and stepped into a dark, putrid passageway that opened onto a vast, natural cavern. A walkway was carved out of the rock and curved around the water's edge; the sea entered through an underwater crevasse and the ground was littered with rotting seaweed and other vegetation. On the far side they could see, what looked like caves, with bars at the openings.

The boys started to run over to them but Charlotte yelled, "STOP!"

The boys froze to the spot just a few feet ahead. What the boys had not seen was the huge head rising out of the water, its three eyes staring at them as it slowly came closer and closer. The top of its head was now ten feet above the water but its mouth was only just visible and it was gnashing its huge, pointy teeth.

Charlotte said quietly, "Walk backwards, slowly; don't make any sudden moves, it can't see you clearly but it can sense you."

The boys did as they were told but the creature kept rising out of the water, by now it was almost fifteen feet tall and it had flippers like a walrus, but the flippers had long claws attached. The creature was flopping across the rotting seaweed, dragging its back half, which seemed not to have any legs or feet. As it got closer and further out of the water, the back half became visible and they saw it was long and snake-like with a spiked tail, which it was using like a whip against the water. The smell was unbearable.

The boys crept back into the passageway and held their noses. How were they going to get past this monster? The creature must have sensed someone in the cells because it was turning its attention there, belly flopping closer and closer until it was outside the middle cell. Its mouth opened and a huge snake-like tongue lashed out through the bars. That's when the kids heard screaming.

"That's Dad, we've got to do something, its trying to kill him!" Nicky yelled and ran out into the open before anyone could stop him.

Jamie ran after him to pull him back but it was too late, the creature had sensed them again and turned its huge head towards them. Its long tongue shot out in their direction, but that wasn't the scariest thing, it had huge spikes on the edge of its tongue and between the spikes were bones of seals and other animals. The boys fell to the ground, just as the tongue whipped over their heads. They got up and started running back to the door; they heard the swish and threw themselves down again.

Jamie, who had fallen onto Nicky, felt a searing pain between his shoulder blades and his mind went foggy; he felt Nicky scrambling up and then he felt himself being tugged at but he couldn't get up. Someone else was grabbing his arm and started pulling him, he tried to help but it was like his legs didn't belong to him, he felt himself being pulled across the wet, slimy ground; he could hear Nicky yelling at him to get up, but it was as if he was far away and when he tried to look at him, he kept disappearing in a fog. Jamie tried again to stand but couldn't feel his legs, the fog was closing in, everything was white and then everything went black and silent.

Nicky and Cali dragged Jamie into the passage, ducking as the tongue shot out again and again; they heard the swish of the tongue and it hit the wall, sending fragments of rock raining down on them. Nicky knelt down beside Jamie to look at his wound, paying little attention to what Charlotte and Cali were saying, all he could see was Jamie's deathly white face and the blood soaking Jamie's sweatshirt. Nicky tore off his own t-shirt and ripped it into bandages, bound Jamie's wound as best he could and finally Jamie looked up at him with blurry eyes and groaning with pain. He pulled the bandages tight to stop the bleeding.

"The only thing we can do is use deadly force," Charlotte was saying, "I can't see any other way to stop it."

"What are you thinking?" Cali asked.

"The Crucify Spell," she answered "But I'm going to need your help, I'm not strong enough on my own. Are you ready Cali?"

Cali nodded and stood beside the cat.

The cat and Cali stepped out into the cavern and yelled, "Crucificare, Crucify!" but the creature still didn't stop.

Cali turned to Nicky and cried, "Nicky we need you, hurry!"

Nicky looked over at them and then back at Jamie, torn between helping them and staying with Jamie. Cali screamed again, "Nicky, you must help us, we can't do this without you, its too strong!" He took one more look at Jamie, who had passed out again, jumped up and ran to them and the three of them yelled, "Crucificare, Crucify!". This time the creature's head crashed to the ground and a huge out-take of air whirled around the cavern like a tornado.

The creature was dead, but Jamie wasn't fairing much better. The cat came over and looked at him. She whispered, very close to his ear, "Heilen" and Jamie slowly opened his eyes; He was very pale but at least he was conscious. Nicky helped him to sit up and lean against the wall, but the cat said, "He'll have to wait for us here, we don't know what else is out there, let's go!"

Jamie nodded and pushed Nicky away and said, "She's right go and get Dad, I'll be fine, GO!"

Nicky reluctantly got up and followed Cali and the cat out into the cave, they carefully made their way around the creature, keeping their eyes on it in case it was just stunned, but it didn't move. They reached the cells and peered into the darkness of the middle cell. They could hear some laboured breathing but couldn't see anything. Nicky whispered, "Dad! Dad! Is that you?"

"Nicky?" said an agonized voice, then, more to himself, "No! it's a trick, how could he be here?"

"Yes! Dad, it's me, we've come to get you!" said Nicky, his emotions almost at the breaking point.

"No, no it's a trick! You want me to tell you where they are, I won't! I won't!" said the voice, now sounding desperate.

"Please Dad, it's it IS ME! Jamie's here too but he got hurt; please come to the door so I can see you," Nicky pleaded.

The cat said, "We don't have time for this, out of the way!" and before Nicky had taken two steps away from the door, she said something and the door flew open. Nicky ran inside and, to his horror, saw the state of his father. He had cuts and bruises all over his face, his left arm lay limp by his side and his clothes were tattered and torn. But worse were his eyes, they were misty white and unfocused, no longer did they shine a dark, sparkling brown like his own. Nicky touched his father gently on the cheek but his father jumped as if he had been slapped. Nicky didn't know what to do, but Charlotte was beside him.

She said, "Mr Elder, you're boys have come to rescue you, please let them!"

"Who's that?" said their father, backing away.

"That's Charlotte, she's a cat right now but she's human, please dad let's go before someone comes!" Nicky pleaded again.

This time Roger Elder staggered to his feet with his hands stretched out in front of him trying to find Nicky. He touched him on the head, felt the curls, and crushed him to him.

"It is you, how did you get here, where's Jamie?"

"He's over in the passageway, he's been hurt; come on let's go!" Nicky said.

Nicky turned in his father's embrace, hanging onto his good arm and putting it over his shoulders, he held him around his waist and led Roger passed the creature and over to the passageway.

Jamie was now standing unsteadily with Cali supporting him; he stepped forward as they reached him and he reached out to his father, saying, "Dad... what did they do to you?"

But there was no time for talking; they had to get back upstairs without anyone finding them. Cali pulled Jamie away from Roger and followed Charlotte. Nicky hung on tightly to Roger, every nerve in his body screaming, his heart pounding so hard he thought it was going to burst, fear of discovery loomed with every step they took but Nicky wasn't about to let fear get the better of him,

"Careful Dad, we've got go up some steps now," Nicky said, guiding his dad up the steps. He staggered under the weight of his father.

"Sorry Nicky I don't have the strength...."

"It's okay, lean on me as much as you want, we're nearly at the top," Nicky panted.

Nicky saw Charlotte peeking around the door. He could hear voices from the passageway and his heart missed a beat, there was nowhere to go but down and he really didn't want to do that again.

Luck was with them though; the voices passed the door and soon couldn't be heard. The gang crept along the passageway back to the empty room. Just as they reached the door a yell came from behind them. Nicky spun around and yelled, "Bindan, Bind!" and the warlock fell to the ground, squirming under the invisible cords. Cali also spun around and recited the Silence Spell, to stop him from yelling.

"Stay here Dad, I'll be right back" Nicky said, leaning his dad against the wall. He and Cali hurried over to the warlock and hid him behind the nearest door. Charlotte and Jamie had already entered the room and Charlotte was climbing through the window when Nicky, once again holding onto Roger, and Cali entered.

But the alarm was raised. As Cali crawled through the window she heard Charlotte use the Stupefying Spell on a warlock who had just ran out in front of her. Cali reached back in and took Roger's good hand and he struggled through the window. She grabbed Jamie around the waist and hauled him to his feet and set off as fast as she could down the path to the beach. Nicky clambered through the window right behind his dad but someone grabbed his leg. Panic gripped him; he could feel himself being pulled back through the window. He flung out his arms to brace himself and kicked as hard as he could; he felt the hand let go and heard the warlock fall. He pulled himself through and slammed the window shut.

"Are you okay, what was that crash?" Roger said, reaching out for Nicky.

"I'm fine, I just knocked some boxes over when I climbed through," Nicky lied. He grabbed his dad around the waist again and together they ran after the others.

Three warlocks jumped out of the bushes as Nicky and his dad passed. Nicky knew they weren't going to be able to outrun them, he reached into his pocket and grabbed the first thing he put his hand on, the vial. It only took him a few seconds to make the decision; he lobbed it over his shoulder but couldn't remember the spell, he looked back and saw the vial smash on the ground and a bright purple mist envelope the warlocks and begin to twist like a tornado and, with a poof of white, they were gone. He looked towards the others running ahead of him; they hadn't seen. But his father had heard.

"What was that?" asked Roger, instinctively looking over his shoulder but unable to see.

"A potion, I threw it at the warlocks so we could get away," Nicky said, trying not to sound too scared. Nicky was thankful his father didn't ask any more questions. Just a few more minutes and they would be on the beach.

Jamie was only vaguely aware of what was going on; he could feel the cold, sea air on his face but Cali was a blur; he could feel his legs moving but he was not in control of them. He stumbled over a tree root and felt Cali hold him up; in the far distance of his mind he could hear his dad talking but couldn't make out what he was saying. There was a small, greyish blur ahead of him which he tried to concentrate on, he knew it was important and he must follow it but for the life of him, he couldn't work out what it was.

There, just in front, was the beach. Jamie and Cali stumbled over to the powerboat just a few more feet ahead of them. Then a flash and another flash! Nicky reached into his pocket for the drawstring bag and pulled out a handful of dust; he threw the bag to Cali who took a handful too. Another flash and another and now four warlocks were descending on them from all directions. Jamie fell into the powerboat and their dad clambered in but they weren't quick enough; a warlock grabbed at Cali, she swung around and blew dust in his face saying, "Stupefacere Stupify" and the warlock stopped moving.

A second later, another warlock grabbed at Cali too but Nicky blew dust into his face and yelled the spell. They managed to push the boat into the water and jumped into it, Nicky turned the key and the engine roared to life. The boat slowly moved away from the beach only to be grabbed by another warlock, but this time the cat lunged at the warlock and dug her claws into his hands. He screamed and fell face first into the water. The boat picked up speed and glided over the choppy, black water heading for the open sea.

But they weren't safe yet; coming around the cove from both directions, were six speedboats racing to block their escape. Just a few more yards and they would be clear. Nicky pressed the throttle and the boat lurched forward, speeding closer and closer to the ever shrinking gap between the speedboats… thirty feet, twenty feet, ten feet; he swung the wheel to the right and then to the left, swerving around one boat and then the other and, a second later, the two speedboats collided head on with a huge explosion that lit up the night sky. The powerboat sped on, Nicky only glancing back for a second to see what had happened.

The dock loomed closer, Cali fumbled in her pocket for a globe and the broomstick. She shoved the pocket globe into Nicky's hand and said, "With only one of you thinking clearly you had better take the pocket globe, touch your finger on Cornwall and say, "Farmer Pearce's Barn", it will take you to the nearest farm to the valley, stay in the barn until someone comes to get you, okay? I'll take Charlotte with me, now go!"

Nicky let go of the steering wheel, hooked arms with his dad and brother and touched Cornwall and said, "Farmer Pearce's Barn" and in a flash they were gone. Cali picked up Charlotte and said, "Entrance to the Valley" and vanished. The boat carried on speeding closer and closer to the dock with the speedboats in hot pursuit, it crashed into the dock. The boats slowed down and the warlocks began searching the water for the escapees.

A dark figure lurking on the dock watched with interest the drama unfolding on the water. He saw the speedboats crash; he saw two boys and a man disappear from the powerboat and then a girl carrying a cat. A smile crossed his face and in a flash of yellow light he disappeared too.

Nicky, Jamie and Roger landed amongst the hay bales in Farmer Pearce's barn. Nicky jumped up, ran to the door and peeked through the crack; they were quite a distance from the farmhouse and probably a mile from the road. He turned back to his dad and brother and wondered what he was going to do. Jamie was deathly white and had passed out again and Dad obviously had a broken arm and was blind. He was searching the hay for Jamie, softly calling his name but getting no answer.

Nicky walked over and said, "He's passed out again, Dad".

"Take me to him, I can't do much but at least I can hold him."

Nicky took his dad's good arm and stretched it over to where Jamie was. His dad moved over and cradled Jamie's head in his lap. Nicky paced backwards and forwards, scared the warlocks would find them and unsure of his ability to deal with them if they did. Sweat was trickling down between his shoulder blades from his soaked curls, he wiped his forehead on the sleeve of his sweatshirt and looked over at his dad and brother. How could he protect them, he was only ten, warlocks were grown men, what was he supposed to do. He turned away, he wanted to scream, "I'm just a kid, I can't do this!". Instead he walked back towards them, listening for any little noise from outside. Inside, only Jamie's uneven breathing broke the silence.

Suddenly there was a flash outside! Nicky ran over to his dad and brother and threw straw over them and told his dad to keep quiet; he hid behind another hay bale, waiting. The barn door creaked open and a voice said, "Don't be afraid, I'm here to help you, my name is Milton Blueblood, I'm a sorcerer, I work for the Council. I'm going to come in so that you can see me; okay?"

Nicky didn't answer; he froze behind the bale watching the door slowly open. A big man, wearing a black, donkey jacket and a flat cap came slowly in. He had frizzy grey hair hanging down to his shoulders.

"I was watching from the dock when you came out of the mist, is Roger Elder okay? Are you his sons?" he said, looking around the barn but not being able to see anyone. Suddenly another flash lit up the barn right beside Nicky, he jumped up but before he could do anything, the man in the donkey jacket yelled, "Bindan Bind" and the newcomer fell over, writhing under the invisible cords.

The big man came over to Nicky and smiled at him, "Are you okay, you look scared stiff, where's your dad and brother?"

"We're over here, but my son isn't doing too well." said Roger sitting up.

Milton Blueblood hurried over and knelt down beside Jamie, he felt his forehead and saw the blood soaked bandages. He looked up at Nicky and tried to smile a re-assuring smile, but he didn't like the look of Jamie.

He got up and said, "We had better keep a lookout, you never know when they will come" and walked over to the door and looked out. Nicky took one more look at Jamie and went to the other end of the barn to watch the back.

It was still dark when Cali and Charlotte popped up in front of the entrance to the valley, to the surprise of the warlocks watching the entrance. She stepped onto the dirt road and vanished again, appearing a second later at the Mansion. She pounded on the front door and didn't stop until a light went on in the Front Hall; a few seconds later the door was opened by Uncle Morton and right behind him were the three sisters.

"We have him, but they're hurt, badly hurt, we've got to get them now, come on, the barn before they catch them!!" she yelled, trying to pull Uncle Morton through the door. Uncle Morton pulled his arm free and grabbed her by the shoulders and said,

"Calm down, we can't understand you, who's got who and who's hurt?"

Cali stopped trying to pull away and said, more calmly, "Mr Elder, we rescued him but Jamie got hurt, and Mr. Elder's hurt too, I gave them a globe 'cos they weren't thinking right, now they're at Pearce's barn, we have to go!" The four adults stood and stared at her until she yelled, "Please, believe me, they're in danger!"

Finally, Constance said, "Amy, get the Pennith's and the doctor! And we're going to need another diversion!"

Morton, Lydia, Constance and Cali grabbed the broomstick and vanished in a flash. A second later they were at the entrance and could see the two warlocks keeping watch across the road; one seemed to be sleeping but the other one was pacing up and down beside the car.

"Okay, we're going to have to step out holding onto the broomstick so we can dematerialise instantly," said Constance.

She looked at Cali, "You should stay here, you've put yourself in enough danger already. Now don't argue!"

Cali had started to protest, but stopped when she realised they hadn't got time for arguing. She stepped away from the broomstick and the others stepped onto the road, an instant later they had vanished. Cali wasn't even sure that the warlock had seen them, as he had been facing the other way at the time. She collapsed on the dew-soaked grass suddenly feeling exhausted, the adrenaline had stopped pumping, she put he hands over her eyes and started to cry.

No sooner had she sat down than Amy, the Pennith's, the doctor and Cali's parents materialised in front of her. Cali's mother grabbed her and started scolding her, but ended up hugging her. Her father was busy talking to Amy, the Pennith's and the doctor. The Pennith's and Cali's father approached the entrance, ran at the warlocks performing the Stupefying Spells as they went. The warlocks, stunned by the sudden onslaught, were taken off guard and were easily dealt with.

* * * *

Constance, Lydia and Morton appeared suddenly beside Nicky. Milton Blueblood spun around ready to do battle but when he saw who it was, acknowledged them with a nod of his head. They didn't waste any time talking, each took out a broomstick from their pockets, Morton and Milton lifted Jamie from the straw and held onto the broomstick, Constance bent down and whispered something in Roger's ear, he scrambled to his feet, she put her arm around his waist and his good arm on the broomstick. Lydia drew Nicky to her, a sympathetic smile on her lips, he reached out and held onto the broomstick. One by one, they disappeared.

Three yellow flashes again and they appeared at the entrance, they stepped over the threshold and were back in the valley. Nicky watched as the doctor bent over Jamie who was, by this time, hardly breathing; he was as white as a sheet and the wound had begun to bleed again.

The doctor asked, "What caused this wound?"

Nicky, choking back a sob, answered, "A great, big sea-monster, with fangs! It just shot out it's tongue and there were spikes on it and…. Jamie fell."

The doctor looked very concerned, "We have to get him to my surgery now."

In a flash he was gone, a second flash and Constance and Roger were gone. Nicky felt very alone; he looked over at Cali standing next to her mother, tears still glistening on her eyelashes and she smiled at him. Milton Blueblood was in deep conversation with Cali's dad. Nicky felt an arm around his shoulder and looked up into Auntie Lydia's caring green eyes, "We had better get you home young man, you've got a lot to answer for!"

"But I want to go with Jamie," Nicky said.

"No, it's best if you go home," she said.

"Please, I need to, it was my fault he got hurt, he was protecting me, please, I must!" Nicky pleaded.

"Very well then, but if your parents say you have to go home, you go home, okay?" she said softly.

Nicky nodded and he and Auntie Lydia held the broomstick and vanished, re-appearing a few seconds later outside of the doctor's surgery. The sun was just peaking over the hills as they entered. Nicky found his parents sitting in the waiting room, a nurse was cleaning up his dad's cuts and bruises. His arm had already been fixed but his eyes were still misty and unfocused. Constance was talking quietly to him, but when Nicky came in she looked over at him and he felt a pang of guilt. She got up and walked over to him, he thought she was going to yell at him, but she pulled him to her and hugged him. He wished she would yell at him, he didn't deserve to be hugged after what had happened to Jamie.

"What were you two thinking, you might have been killed, and whatever possessed you to act on your own? The Council was working on it!" she said.

"Cali's dad said the Council didn't know what to do and that Ostrogoth was going to kill Dad, so we had to do it, we've been practicing spells for ages," Nicky answered, glad he could explain.

"What do you mean practicing spells, what kind of spells?" she said, her anger rising.

"Just ones that would help us to get Dad back, but we did have to use a deadly one against the sea monster, because it was hurting Dad and we couldn't get to him," Nicky said quietly, realising how feeble his excuses were.

The doctor entered the room with a big book in his hands; he walked over to Nicky and said gently, "Is this the creature that hurt Jamie?"

Nicky looked down at the drawing of the creature they had killed and nodded. The doctor looked up with a worried expression on his face.

He said, "This is a very old creature and the spikes on its tongue are poisonous. Depending on how much poison entered Jamie's system and how long ago, will make all the difference, I've given him an antidote but it's not exactly for this creature, it's for one of his smaller cousins, so it may or may not work. I'm sorry".

Constance fell into a chair, put her hands over her eyes, and began to sob quietly. Nicky just stood there staring at the doctor; this wasn't right, no-one was meant to get hurt, they were just meant to rescue their dad and be heroes. Now Jamie was lying in the other room fighting for his life, just because he had saved him, Nicky, from the monster.

Nicky turned and ran as fast as he could out of the surgery, he heard Lydia calling after him but he didn't stop, he had to find Charlotte. He ran all the way to the Mansion, let himself in by the front door and headed down to the cellar. He found

Charlotte lying in front of the fire, still a cat. She looked up as he came running in.

"What's happened?" she asked feebly.

"Jamie's dying, that thing's spikes on its tongue were poisonous and it's all my fault, we've got to save him!" Nicky cried.

"How can we save him, if the doctor can't?" she said, rising slowly and walking over to him.

"The crystal, we could find the crystal?" Nicky said helplessly.

"Where do we start, I've been here a hundred years and haven't found it," she said.

Nicky thought for a few minutes and then said. "When I first came down here, I got a strange feeling when I was in the first chamber".

He picked up the lamp from the table and they hurried out into the bigger chamber and started frantically looking around. Nicky began to get the feeling that everything was all right, but he shook it off and continued to look. Charlotte, who was still a cat, began to sniff and Nicky desperately scanned the stonewalls. Charlotte had a scent and was walking to the deepest corner of the chamber. Nicky followed her; she stopped and looked at the wall.

"This feels like the right place, but I don't see anything," she said.

Nicky looked quickly up and down the wall and then a stone caught his eye, scratched into it, was a P intertwined with a C, he had seen this before, where? Then it came to him; on the rings that his aunt and Mrs. Pennith wore. He grabbed a stick from the ground and began to chip away at the crumbling mortar between the stones, but Charlotte said "Nicky, that will take you forever, go to the cupboard where I keep the spell books, you'll find a very old book called, "A History of the Padstows". Bring it to me"

Nicky ran off to the other chamber, found the book and carried it back to Charlotte.

"Open it to the middle page, there should be a loose piece of paper there, be very careful it's extremely old and fragile"

Nicky opened the book and found the piece of paper, he unfolded it carefully and looked at the handwriting, it was very faded and barely legible.

"That is the spell that has been handed down to the eldest heir, it was written by Simon after he hid the crystal. You, being an heir, should be able to open the wall."

Nicky looked back down at the piece of crumbling paper and read;

"Here I stand, a descendent and rightful heir to the house of Padstow.

Through torture and pain, I will not reveal the resting place.

Forever to be hidden from sight until a need, once again, brings to light.

To hold me to the highest degree, strike me down if I am not what I decree

Now upon my oath I do avow, my need is great, the crystal be revealed."

The wall, once in shadow, now glowed as if a spotlight was on it, the stones shimmered like water and melted away to reveal another chamber. Nicky asked Charlotte for the lamp sitting on the floor beside her.

"I can't change at the moment dear," she said feebly.

"What's wrong, are you going to stay a cat?" Nicky asked with concern in his voice.

"I don't know dear," Charlotte said, laying down beside the lamp. Nicky bent down and looked at her "Go dear, Jamie needs you more than I do." Nicky picked up the lamp and entered the chamber.

The chamber was long and narrow. On one side were archways with wrought iron gates between them and behind these were large flat stones engraved with the names and dates of the Padstows. The nearest one had a stone carving of John Padstow laid out with his hands crossed on his chest and, at his head, as if watching over him, was a large golden hawk. On the wall behind the tomb were his name and the date he was born and the date he died. The others weren't as elaborate as John's, but they all had brass plaques with their names and dates. The tombs went on and on, all behind gates. Nicky held up the lamp but couldn't see the end, he walked along looking at the tombs until he came to one that had two pedestals instead of tombs behind the gate and, as the light from his lamp hit the magnificent crystal sitting atop one of the pedestals, prisms in greens, blues, yellows, pinks and purples flooded the chamber.

Nicky yelled to Charlotte, "You have to see this, it's beautiful!" and slowly Charlotte raised her aching body up off the floor and made her way to Nicky's side She stood there soaking up the healing powers of the crystal and soon she was able to move without hurting. Nicky had moved to the gate and was looking up at the cantaloupe-sized crystal. He tried to open the gate but it was locked and the hinges looked to be rusted shut.

"Now what am I going to do, I've found the Crystal but I can't get to it?" he said desperately.

"Give me a second," Charlotte said, crawling between the bars and, once on the other side, began to transform. She reached up, gently took down the crystal, and walked over to the gate, but it wouldn't fit between the bars. She tried to push it underneath but it wouldn't fit there either. They stood back and looked for a way of getting the Crystal to Nicky.

Nicky hurried over to the next gate to see if it was the same; it was but one of the bars looked rusted through. He gave it a few good yanks and it broke off and clattered to the ground. Charlotte came over and pushed the Crystal through, then changed back and crawled through the bars.

"Hurry off to the doctors, Jamie needs you, I'll see you when you get back."

Nicky stuffed the Crystal inside his coat and ran off. He glanced back and saw the cat lying on the floor, not moving; Nicky went back and asked, "Are you okay?" She didn't say anything and Nicky gently picked her up, cradled her in his arms and carried her back to the fireplace where he laid her on her chair.

"I'll be back as soon as I can with the Crystal and then you can change back again," he said gently. The cat slowly nodded her head, laid it over her paws, and closed her eyes. Nicky ran out of the mansion. By now the sun had risen high in the sky and the birds were singing happily in the trees. Nicky ran as fast as he could all the way to the doctor's surgery.

He arrived to see Auntie Lydia being comforted by Uncle Morton, who was trying hard to fight back the tears. When they saw Nicky coming they tried to stop him.

"I've got to go and help Jamie!" he said struggling to get away.

"It's too late dear, Jamie died ten minutes ago," said Uncle Morton softly.

"No, I can save him, LET ME GO, I'VE GOT TO GET IN THERE!" he screamed and tried to pull himself away again.

"There's nothing you can do to save him Nicky, it's too late, the doctor did everything he could," said Uncle Morton kindly but more firmly

"BUT I'VE FOUND THE CRYSTAL, it will save him!"

This time he broke free, ran into the surgery, and found the room where Jamie lay. He saw his mum and dad leaning over Jamie sobbing. The doctor was standing against the wall talking to the nurse. His mum looked up, tears were rolling down her cheeks, the doctor started forward but Nicky reached under his coat, pulled out the Crystal and ran over to Jamie, holding the crystal over him. But he didn't know what he was meant to do, no one had told him how it worked! He looked pleadingly from his mum to the doctor and back to his mum.

His mother realised what he was trying to do and held onto the Crystal also. As the doctor walked over to the bed, he said, "Is that THE crystal?" Nicky didn't answer. Nicky and his mother guided the Crystal up and down Jamie's body watching for any signs of life. The seconds ticked by with no sign.

"What's happening, someone please tell me?" Roger begged. Lydia and Morton had followed Nicky in and Auntie Amy came in, wiping her eyes. When Lydia and Amy saw what they were trying to do, they hurried over and held onto the Crystal too. Nicky, crying softly, was saying, "Please Jamie, wake up, please Jamie, please, please!"

The Crystal began to glow from an inner light source and prisms started to dance around the people holding it. A warm, soft light shone down onto Jamie and grew brighter and brighter until it consumed his whole body. As everyone looked down at him, the colour started to return to his face, his chest gently rose and fell, his mouth opened, and he took a gulp of air. His eyes blinked open and he looked at the tear-streaked faces of his family above him. The bright light dulled to a warm glow and slowly the prisms faded away.

"Is he alright, tell me, is that him breathing?" Roger asked and felt Jamie's hand squeeze his.

"Yes dear, he's breathing, Nicky found the Padstow Crystal and brought it to us to rejuvenate him, he's going to be fine" Constance answered, crying now with happiness.

Chapter Fifteen

A New Beginning

The village was abuzz with the story of the rescue of Roger Elder by his sons and Cali Pendoggett, also of the discovery of the Padstow Crystal, which had brought Jamie back to life and restored Roger Elder's sight. What they didn't know was that it had also brought Charlotte back from the brink of death too.

Returning to the manor with the Crystal, Nicky had slipped down to the cellar to find the cat still curled up on the armchair where he had laid her, but her breathing was laboured. He held the Crystal over her and she began to breathe easier. After about an hour she was able to transform back into the old lady. She told him that the adventure had been too much, even for her cat body and, without the Crystal; she would not have made it. Nicky decided right then and there that the only place for the Crystal was in Charlotte's chamber so that she could use it whenever she needed it, because she deserved it, for if it wasn't for her, they wouldn't have got their dad back and without her senses, he wouldn't have found the Crystal to save Jamie. But Charlotte said the only place for the Crystal was where it had always been and if she needed it, she now knew how to get to it. So the crystal was returned to the pedestal and the wall sealed itself up once again.

Now when the boys go into the village, everyone greets them fondly and, a few days ago, Mr Pickerall at the Hardware Shop even came out to greet them and gave Nicky the penknife he had been looking at. Cali too, was a celebrity in the village, but only after her mother had punished her by not allowing her out of her sight for a week and even then she had to promise that she and the boys wouldn't do anything so dangerous again.

One of the old men in the village stopped the three kids one sunny afternoon after they had brought an ice cream cone from the newsagents. He handed them each a small package and when they were opened, they found rings exactly like the ones their mum and aunts wore. When asked about them, the old man told them that his family had been making the rings for hundreds of years and that P and C stood for Padstow Crystals. Anyone wearing one was either a Padstow by birth or they had done something brave in the name of the Padstows. They thanked the old man, slipped the rings onto their fingers, and admired them as they ate their ice creams.

And today, returning to the mansion, the boys were informed that there was going to be a family meeting after supper that night and the boys were invited to join in. At seven o'clock they all gathered in the kitchen with their cups of tea and biscuits.

Roger Elder began by saying, "I know I'm an outsider here, what you call a Normal, but if it wasn't for the gift that my boys inherited from their mother I don't think I would be here now and I just want to say, thank you to all of you for coming to my rescue and risking your lives for me, and especially my boys. I will never be able to repay the debt, so whatever you decide is fine with me".

The boys looked at each other, then around the table, not quite understanding what their father meant, until their mother said, "Your aunts and uncle and I have been talking and if everyone is agreeable, I think we should move back to the valley, it's too dangerous for us out there with Cyrus Ostrogoth still after the Crystal".

"We have decided" Lydia said, "We can split the house into living areas so that we're not living in each others pockets. It will take some money but now that the Crystal has been found, things should look up for us."

"We can use that spell to fix all the broken furniture on the third floor and sell it at market, it's so old it must be antique and antiques are worth lots of money, right?" Nicky said excitedly.

Everyone smiled and nodded.

"Which part of the manor are we going to live in?" asked Jamie.

"The north wing as there are four of us, it will take some fixing but I think the four of us can handle it, and the mason in the village has offered to fix the wall for free and we can get glass for the windows from the town and some of the women in the village have offered to help clean, which shouldn't be too difficult with our secret, eh boys?" Constance said winking at the boys.

"What about Dad's job and the police?" Nicky asked.

"I've contacted the police, I told them I escaped and had no idea why they kidnapped me. My boss has also given me a leave of absence for as long as I want and also offered me a position in the Exeter office, but for now, I'm going to stay here with you and get to know my boys, maybe you can teach me some spells?" Roger said, with a sparkle in his brown eyes.

"There's another matter that needs to be discussed." Nicky said, getting up and walking to the back door, He opened it to allow the grey tabby cat to enter. "I would like to introduce you to Charlotte Whitehaven."

The cat slowly grew bigger and bigger, the grey fur turned into white hair and an old-fashioned, grey dress; the paws became feet and hands. Charlotte looked at their shocked faces, smiled and said, "It's nice to finally meet you all in person."

They all tried to speak at once but Nicky quieted them, explained the whole story to them, and then said,

"Charlotte would like to continue living in the cellar with the Crystal, also she doesn't want anyone else to know about her yet, okay?"

They nodded in agreement and Charlotte finally sat down at the table with her family.

"I think there's one more thing we should discuss," Jamie said, "and that's changing the name back to its original name. I say we call our home "Padstow Mansion" All in favour say 'Aye!'"

There was a unanimous "Aye!"

The End